Whose Life Is It Anyway?

DAVID BENEDICTUS

SPHERE BOOKS LIMITED
30/32 Gray's Inn Road, London WC1X 8JL

First published in 1981 by Sphere Books Ltd and
George Weidenfeld & Nicolson Ltd
This novelisation copyright © 1981 David Benedictus
Based on material copyright © 1981 Metro-Goldwyn-Mayer
Film Co. and Amber Lane Productions Ltd.

Set in Century Schoolbook

Printed and bound in Great Britain by
Cox & Wyman Ltd, Reading

PROLOGUE
RIDING HIGH

Air and light and space.

As a boy he had watched the sea-gulls soaring, turning on a skate's heel, resting on the wind, plummeting to the sea, and had marvelled at their grace and agility. He had watched for so long that his mother had become anxious. Was it natural? Was it *natural*! There was nothing so natural as a sea-gull. His father thought a baseball was natural; and Coca Cola.

Air and light and space.

Pat was so light that he could lift her with one hand. Sometimes he would put a Herbie Mann disc on the turntable and she would dance to the flute music. Watching her dance, she reminded him of the sea-gulls. She appeared so delicate that he was terrified that when he lay on top of her and thrust into her he might crumple her. She would be too fragile, too brittle for a heavy bearded fellow like him, and he would have speared her to death.

Air and light and space.

He loved Concorde. Other machines were efficient, adaptable, labour-saving, but other machines were earthbound, lumpish things without any grace to them. His sculptures were all to do with sea-gulls and Pat and Concorde. They soared, they turned on a skate's heel, they rested on the wind, they danced, they received

3

him into them, they flew at many times the speed of sound.

He was on a hydraulic lift which he could raise to the top of his massive steel sculpture, but it was inefficient, raised him only slowly, let him down with a bump. He felt unworthy of the sculpture he had created, like a computer programmer outwitted at chess by his own programme. He wore a welder's mask and heavy protective gloves, and wielded an acetylene torch. Such things made him feel less of an artist, made him feel clumsy. But without them his imagination would have no room to grow. This sculpture, the biggest he had yet attempted, justified it all. It scintillated against the blue Bostonian sky. It made Ken feel that he was a little more than human. One day he would create a perfect cone of stainless steel. It would be so strong that it would survive cold and heat, flood and hurricane; it would be taller than Everest. It would be without purpose.

So was this sculpture; except that it was intended for the pleasure of children.

He called down to his students. Was the final beam secured? Were they confident that the timber had been bolted, and would hold? They shouted back that they were. Pat stood amongst them, very tiny, in a blue coat over a check waistcoat. Her hair shone and loose strands of it moved in the wind. She looked about twelve, very happy, without adult anxieties. She smiled up at him. He was very lucky, to love her, and to have her.

Really, the sculpture was finished. He hated to

4

admit it, because once it was complete it would no longer belong to him, but to the world, though whether the world would want it ... He pressed the button to descend.

Back on the grass he removed his protective armour and ran his hands through his hair. He was all over grease and sweat. Two-dimensional artists did not realise how lucky they were. There were some children standing around watching. He called to them:

'Use it,' but they seemed nervous of him and stayed where they were. He nodded to his students to gather up the tools. Then:

'Use it,' he called again. Goddam kids!

He swung on a beam and eased himself through a narrow crevice. The children watched him as though he had just descended from outer space, which, in a sense, he had. Pat ran over to him and clutched his arm. He wanted to kiss her, but she was so clean ...

'It's really beautiful, Ken.'

'It should be. You were the model.'

A couple of the braver children had begun to explore it gingerly.

'That's right, use it. Don't be scared.'

Pat said, 'What if they damage it before the dedication?'

'This *is* the dedication.'

The students were chattering excitedly, taking photographs, gesturing in the air. He joked with them, reminding them that there would be no extra credit for any of this, that their term papers had to be in by Wednesday, that their spelling and writing had better improve.

The children were overcoming their inhibitions. It really was for them? It was. They explored it. It was full of possibilities.

'I was the model for *that*?' Pat asked in amazement.

'Only the round bits.'

'Boy,' said Pat grimly, 'are you gonna get it.'

'Promises, promises.'

Pat had to go straight on to ballet class. She would be home, she said, at six. It would be Ken's turn to get the supper. Supper for Pat – that was a contradiction in terms. Celery and cottage cheese and low-calorie Coke would be a banquet for her. Ken sighed. He had been working hard. He had images of Lobster Newburg and cheese-cake; some chance!

He watched Pat go. He would forgive her her dietary fads; maybe he would treat himself to a slice of pizza, a secret between himself and his stomach. He climbed into his sports car and drove off. The air was cool, the sun reflected off the chrome. Air and light and space.

He waited at an intersection, and thought about the completed sculpture. It had not been a major commission, but he had completed it on schedule and within budget. He was a professional. He looked at his hands. Grimy, but strong. Strong, but subtle. He loved the feel of things, of wire, of clay, of wood, of metal. Even this steering wheel. The lights changed to green.

Halfway across the intersection, a truck the

6

size of a small house hit Ken's sports car broadside. Ken never saw it.

No air. No light. No space.

There were lights; blues, reds, yellows, flashing and turning. It was like a carnival. There were whistles and sirens and the distorted voices of closed circuit radios. It was like a madhouse. There were cops and firemen and ambulance men and a crowd of onlookers fascinated and relieved. Fascinated at what could happen so quickly to somebody else. Relieved at what should now not happen to them. It was spectacular.

The truck driver was explaining that his brakes had failed. He kept on saying it, as though, if they did not believe him at first, they would be bound to believe him in the end. The crowd thought it rare and strange to see such a big man in tears.

The paramedic was putting an oxygen mask over Ken's face. He talked to him gently and assured him that everything would be all right.

The firemen were cutting away at Ken's car with hacksaws and crowbars; sometimes with their bare hands. They had seen it all before, but this, man, this was bad.

Another paramedic listened to Ken's heart with a stethoscope. He was in the firemen's way, but the firemen waited for him to finish. Having listened to Ken's heart, he searched for Ken's arm, rolled up the sleeve, wiped the skin with alcohol, injected him. A knowledgeable woman in the crowd whispered to a friend that that was a hopeful sign, that they wouldn't bother to do that if the man were dead.

'Better if he was,' said the friend gloomily.

Ken saw nothing of the carnival, heard nothing of the madhouse, knew nothing of the crowd. As the truck hit him, he had thought: 'What will Pat do for supper?' That was all he had time to think. The oxygen, the injection, the firemen, all the things they were doing to keep him alive, he knew nothing of. He lay as if dead.

He was lifted out of the jagged remains of his car onto a stretcher, oxygen mask over his face, blood dripping into his arm, blankets sheltering his shocked body. Across the road a child, wide-eyed, wondered.

Acutely traumatised, Ken was rushed away in an ambulance. The wrecker removed what was left of his car with altogether less ceremony.

One part of him was aware of the voices. 'He's cyanotic. BP 60/20, pulse 140 and irregular. Expected time of arrival 1320 hours ... Get him on our oxygen and send for Neuro and triage ... ventilate him ... Get me one gram of Solumedrol ... two units of plasma ... type and match ...' The rest of him was floating ... air and light and space ... no pain ... no pain ... he was a sea-gull ... he was dancing ...

The pain came when consciousness fully returned. Ken could still feel the weight pressing down on him. His first thought was that

8

the sculpture had collapsed upon him, but that was ridiculous, it was securely anchored and would withstand any stress or pressure that could be made upon it. The city regulations ensured that. Then he recalled the huge truck which suddenly obscured the light ... *it was still there*! He tried to raise himself, but could not do so. The pain became acute. In his legs, in his arms, in his pelvis, in his ribs, in his stomach, and - intolerably - in his head. He tried to cry out. There was something damp on his upper arm. Then there was nothing.

This time, no floating, no flying, no air, no space, no light. It was as if he were dead.

Aeons later, in another world, in another era, in another dimension, he opened his eyes and saw a familiar pair of shoes. The shoes were familiar, but they were above his head. Now that was not right. However there was comfort to be had from a familiar pair of shoes.

But then there were unfamiliar voices.

'Okay, ready?'

'Yes, man, ready.'

'Straps tight?'

'Tight, yes.'

'Okay, turn.'

And his world turned. (Somebody has turned his Stryker bed.) Suddenly a white expanse of ceiling with lights, like at the dentist, gazing down at him. Between him and the lights comes Pat's face, a blessed sight.

'Hi.'

'Hi.'

She puts her lips to his. They are soft and warm; nothing else in his life is as soft and warm as Pat's lips. Her tongue touches his for a moment, and withdraws.

'Thought those shoes looked familiar,' says Ken.

'Wore them just for you.'

But they are not alone. You're never alone in an Intensive Care Unit. (Much good it would do him if they were.)

'Dizzy?' the nurse asks. 'Want anything?'

'How about a Martini?' It is difficult for Ken to speak. It is almost as though he has forgotten how. Each word has to be taken out of the memory bank, dusted down, tested on the tongue. It is like he is using each word for the very first time. The nurse puts a glass containing a curved straw to Ken's mouth. He sips. The taste is of hospitals. He says:

'Gin tastes like water.'

'It is water.'

'Doesn't everyone in Intensive Care get gin?'

'Sure. Intravenously.'

As he sips, and talks, and jokes, surreptitiously, beneath the blanket, Ken is flexing his muscles. He tries them all in turn. He can feel nothing. Nothing moves. There is no longer any pain. But they have drilled holes into the plate of his skull, and inserted tongs into the holes. The tongs they have connected to a chest collar, so that even his head is firmly fixed. He panics. Pat sees the panic in his eyes, and sees him fighting to control it, sees with pride how he wins the fight. She takes hold of his

10

hand. It does nothing for him, of course, but comforts Pat a little.

'About that dinner-dance next Saturday,' says Ken. 'Maybe you should tell them we'll be late.'

'Okay,' says Pat. But it really isn't okay. Not at all.

PART 1
ACCIDENT PRONE

The months pass. In the real world the seasons change, and now, as the maples burn up the New England hills, in the hospital all is as it always has been, and always will be. Ken, though not as he has always been, is also as he always will be.

He has been removed from the Stryker bed, from the Intensive Care Unit, from the bandages and the casts. They have freed his head too. He has been taken to a private room which has been painted white, because white is supposed to be an optimistic colour. There are even windows, looking out onto the real world, but the windows are never opened, so it's just an illusion. One wall is made of glass, and through it may be seen the nurses' station in Intensive Care. Above Ken's bed is a television camera on continuous duty. Ken can see the nurses by turning his head. The nurses anywhere in the hospital can see Ken on the monitoring screens. Everybody can see everybody. But when the nurses go home and they turn off the lights ...

Here is Rodriguez now. Rodriguez is truly extraordinary. She looks much like a grizzly bear, if one could get a black bear to dress up in a nurse's uniform and pull on rimless glasses. Puerto Rico's loss is Boston's gain, where Rodriguez is concerned. With Rodriguez is a student nurse. Ken has seen them come and go. This one is prettier than most, and looks innocent. Her eyes are clear. Amazing, Ken thinks, that innocence survives at all in the city of the Strangler, a city where children must not speak to strangers, where political corruption is a way of life, where . . .

'Good morning, Mr Harrison,' says Rodriguez, 'here's a new face for you.'

'Fantastic. Hello, new face.'

'Hello,' says the girl shyly, not looking directly at him.

'Rodriguez, why don't you bring me ugly old bags?'

Rodriguez turns the crank at the side of the bed, and Ken's upper half is gradually lowered into the same plane as his lower half.

'Going down! Second floor, Neurology, Gynaecology. Main floor, Ladies Underwear, Rubber Goods . . .'

Rodriguez motions to the new nurse and instructs her to help turn back the sheets and the spread. There are pillows supporting him under his arms. When the girl removes them his arms flop onto the bed; dead meat.

'Rodriguez, why don't you say something nice to her?'

'You need a haircut,' says Rodriguez to him, not to the girl, who has a marvellous head of curls, not as tight or as black as Rodriguez's, but more enticing.

'Oh, that's nice. My hair is all over the place, my beard is all over my face.'

'Get the lotion from the cart and rub him,' says Rodriguez.

'Rub me,' agrees Ken.

'I see any bedsores, it's gonna be you and me, you dig?'

But Rodriguez can find no bedsores. For this tiny triumph Ken is almost proud of his poor, useless body.

'I used to dream of situations like this. Of being massaged by two gorgeous women, of –'

'Lay off,' says Rodriguez, 'or I'll keep my student nurses out of here.' But behind her glasses she is twinkling. A nurse from the Intensive Care Unit taps on the glass and summons Rodriguez.

She asks the new girl, 'Can you manage?'

'Yes, ma'am.'

'Well be careful, we don't want to have him on the floor.'

'Oh God,' says Ken in a desperate croak. 'Somebody have me on the floor. I was once had on the floor.' (It was true. It was Pat. The second time they went out, when they came home.) 'It was incredible.'

The new girl has placed Ken on his side, facing away from her. She has untied the back of his robe. He can smell her faintly, a rather sweet scent – violets; and the lotion; and other things. He can never get used to talking to walls.

'What's your name?'

'Mary Jo Sadler, but my friends call me Joey.'

Her voice is husky. It goes with the scent.

'Don't let Rodriguez hear you say that. You are supposed to answer "Miss Sadler" with a smile full of warmth but no hint of sex.'

'I'm sorry, Mr Harrison.'

'Don't be. I'll call you Joey when we're alone and you're caressing my backside.'

'I'm rubbing your heels right now.'

'Don't spoil it for me! I can dream, can't I?' A sudden onrush of wretchedness threatens to overwhelm Ken. Now he is glad that he is not facing the girl. He continues in as normal a voice as he can muster.

'Am I your first backrub, Joey?'

'You are. I graduate in two weeks.'

'And you can't wait to get here full-time, can you?'

'Right.'

'Students are all the same.'

'Were you a teacher?'

Ken laughs bitterly. 'Never, never use the past tense. You should have said "Are you a teacher?" You are part of the optimism industry now. You are supposed to act as though, for the first time in medical history, a broken spinal cord will heal itself. "We just have to give it time, Mr Harrison." Well?'

Ken has heard the knock on the door, and recognised it. Nobody else knocks like that. Lightly, with the back of the knuckles, delicately, like everything she does. For Pat's benefit, he says:

'Oh God, Joey, quick, under the bed. It's that other woman.'

To Pat, he says softly, 'Hello, chickee.'

She crosses to the bed. She is wearing a long cardigan of heavy-knit Arran wool over black leotards and carries a loose bunch of white chrysanthemums that look as though they've been plucked from an overgrown garden. An amazing woman ... The amazing woman kisses him, but it's a public sort of kiss.

He asks her: 'Rehearsal?'

'Recital.' And then to Mary Jo: 'Does he ever stop?' Mary Jo is embarrassed. She reckons she can handle single men, even the ones with the full use of their limbs, but men and wives together . . .

'Stop what?' says Ken, enjoying the teasing. 'I haven't laid a hand on her.'

'I don't know,' says Mary Jo. 'It's my first day with him.'

'You'll learn.' And Pat introduces herself to Mary Jo.

'She couldn't keep her hands off me,' says Ken. 'Her and that Rodriguez creature. Insatiable both.'

'Look what I've brought you.' Pat presents the flowers to Ken as if she is the manager of La Scala and Ken is Maria Callas, but then, with less ceremony, she removes old flowers from a vase, and replaces them with the chrysanthemums.

Rodriguez bustles back in, greets Pat, gives a critical glance at the bed but can find nothing very much wrong with it, and cranks it up.

'A tat higher?'

'A tat,' says Ken, liking her as always.

'Miss Rodriguez,' says Pat. 'You promised you wouldn't send any more cute ones in here.'

'You think Mary Jo is cute? You should've seen last night's. After lights out, she snuck me out through the laundry chute – quite a ride! And we went skate-boarding. Only problem was that I was the skate-board.'

Having established that Mary Jo has finished rubbing, Rodriguez rolls Ken onto his back and replaces the pillows under his limp arms. Then she and Mary Jo tuck the sheets neatly round him, arrange his arms and hands on top of the sheets. Ken looks at his hands and, anticipating nothing, tries to remember how he activated each finger. Each had a separate muscle and one could see them twitch under the skin of the forearm. Three joints to each finger, two to each thumb. A nail, protected by the quick, and featuring a smoky moon, to each finger. When the brain directed them, they were capable, these powerful yet sensitive tools, of miracles of creation. They could clutch, press, mould, tap, squeeze, pinch, caress. Ken looks from the fingers of his dead hands to Pat. She is watching him, and cannot conceal the pain. Too briskly, she gets up from her chair and (with long, tapering, dancer's fingers) deftly rearranges the flowers in the vase. Too cheerfully she smiles and kisses Ken. Too predictably she says:

'I've got to get back to work out a bit of choreography before the recital. Kallis is coming to the studio. He's still interested in that large nude ...'

'Kallis,' says Ken, 'was always interested in large nudes.'

'So I must run.' Ken wants to tell her that he knows how much it hurts her to be with him, that he would understand if she chose not to come again. 'But I'll see you tomorrow,' she adds, and kisses him gently and sweetly. Ken would have pushed her away if he could have; instead he manages a joke. 'I'll probably be here tomorrow.' But it's not much of a joke. Pat goes.

'All right,' says Rodriguez in her tight lipped nurse's voice, for she is, after so many years'

20

experience, very much aware of 'atmosphere,' 'let's get this show on the road. Are you comfortable, Mr Harrison?'

'Rodriguez, you give great sheet.'

Mary Jo blushes. Great to see a girl blush, thinks Ken, who had no idea they still did. She looks up, sees him watching her, and the blush assumes the proportions of the aurora borealis.

'Okay,' says Rodriguez, 'go to sleep, or something.'

'What's the "or something"?'

'Stay awake.'

Later, in the canteen, Mary Jo asks how long Ken has been in the hospital. Five months says Rodriguez. Then Mary Jo asks the question. And Rodriguez shakes her head. Mary Jo bites her lip.

'Yes,' says Rodriguez, 'me too.'

*   *   *

'Watch out, it's a black man with a razor,' says Ken.

'Holy shit, it's a white man with a problem,' says John.

Now this John is a young, black orderly who moves around the hospital like it was his own back yard. Ken often feels that if the authorities in the hospital began to bear down upon him – and there are hints that they might – John would be the one to turn to; a natural anarchist and a most disorderly orderly.

John wears a bandeau to keep his flowing locks

from flowing, but he operates his electric razor with care and gentleness. Ken trusts him. As the razor whines over Ken's face, John says:

'Okay, turkey, let's see you tap dance. But man, this shaving dudes is dead boring. They don't let me near the chicks.'

'The ones with moustaches?'

'Bitchy, bitchy.'

'No. Envy, envy. From where I'm lying if I could make it at all by myself, that would be great.' Wouldn't it just, thinks Ken. He had asked Emerson about it. Emerson had explained that he could feel desire (he didn't need to be told that) but only in the head. It was to do with the endocrine glands. There could be no ejaculation. And to think he'd been worried about coming too soon. Those whom the gods wish to destroy they first make horny. Not even, he had asked Emerson with something close to panic, in my sleep? Emerson had shaken his head.

'You got it,' says John, unplugging his razor. 'Hey, how's that punk band of yours thriving?'

'Way out. I added a xylophone.'

'A punk xylophone? This I have got to hear.'

'And so you shall.' With which John taps out a rhythm on Ken's ribs while singing:

Punkette nights and pretty lights
Love them ladies dressed in white.

(Ladies in white, thinks Ken, how I could have loved them.)

22

Thursday may be awful sweet
But Friday's dancing time for me
On my feet (feet, feet, feet)
On my feet (feet, feet, feet)

(Dancing with Pat, thinks Ken, was like dancing with one's shadow.)

Punkette nights and pretty lights
Love them ladies dressed in white.

(Oh Christ, thinks Ken, how will I bear it?)

The sweetest girl I ever saw
Is my baby when she's in the raw
In the raw (raw, raw, raw)
In the raw (raw, raw, raw)

Pat - the first time he saw her naked - was so
elegant. In the life class they had always talked of
the infinite variety of the human body, and the
models seemed to have been selected to prove the
point. But nothing had prepared him for Pat. If he
had painted her as he had seen her that first time
they would have called him sentimental.

Punkette nights and pretty lights
Love them ladies dressed in white.

Nicely on cue, Dr Scott comes in. She wears a white coat over a smokey blue blouse and is, despite being a doctor, another fine-looking lady. She seems surprised and even a little alarmed at seeing an orderly playing punk xylophone on her patient's ribs.

'Oh, mama,' John mutters under his breath.

'He was just, em, testing my reflexes.'

'This man's toe-bone is connected to his knee-bone, and I am connecting myself to another patient,' and John sidles towards the door. Then he moves so fast he creates a vacuum, and the door slams shut to fill it.

'What was all *that* about?' Doctor Scott wants to know.

'He was shaving me. Had to look my best for the Chief Resident in Medicine.'

'We're all bright and chipper this morning.'

'Oh, it's marvellous, the courage of the human spirit. Joan of Arc, Thomas More, Martin Luther King, Ken Harrison.'

'Nice to hear the human spirit's okay. How's the heart?' She puts the stethoscope to his chest. Ken fools around.

'You know what a stethoscope is?' he asks her when she has heard all she wants to of his heart. 'A tube with a victim at either end.'

'We're planning to step up your physical therapy starting today.'

'Oh yes?' Ken's voice is suddenly harsh. 'To what purpose?'

'To what purpose? To make you more comfortable and to get you living a more normal life.'

'Meaning I can resume my baseball career?'

Later in the nurses' station, Dr Scott confides in

Rodriguez that she is concerned about the patient Harrison. He seems to be growing more bitter daily. In Rodriguez's view he is beginning to realise what he is up against. Scott decides to increase his daily Valium intake to five milligrams. From his bed, Ken can see them talking and suspects that he is the subject of their conversation.

'If I had wings,' he says ever-so-quietly to himself, 'I would fly away from here.'

*   *   *

It is later that same day, and Doctor Michael Emerson is on his rounds accompanied by four third-year students. Emerson is formidable, walks fast, so that the others have trouble in keeping up with him; he talks fast too.

The group enters a ward where a first-year intern is disconnecting a crash-cart from a corpse. The corpse belongs (belonged until recently) to a middle-aged man with receding sandy hair. The corpse's expression is neither anxious nor peaceful; it is scarcely an expression at all. His face is very white.

'How long?' Emerson asks the intern.

'Twelve minutes.'

'What did you do?'

'Palpated radial artery. Gave him DJW Lasix and Lidocaine.'

'Why didn't you transfer him to Intensive Care?'

'The patient's vitals were stable at six o'clock. He went sour real fast.'

The more observant of the students notice a flicker of pain in Emerson's eyes. He crosses to the foot of the bed, where the chart sets out, in unemotional medical terms, the tragedy of a wasted life. Emerson reads it out to his students:

'Andrew Dryer, age fifty-six. Surgery yesterday. C.A. through the colon, liver. Stapholococcus widespread, pulmonary complications. Could anything have been done for him?' The cubicle is silent. Then, unexpectedly, one of the students yawns. Emerson turns his craggy face from the dead to the living.

'What's your name?'

'Everett, sir.'

'Well, Mr Everett, tell us how do you feel about this?'

'Feel, sir?'

'Yes, feel. Do you perhaps feel sick when you look at this?'

'No, sir.'

'Why not?'

'I'm used to seeing bodies, sir.'

Emerson smiles grimly at him. Everett wonders what he has said that was out of place.

'Oh, you are ...? You've been here, what, three years? Cut up cadavers with the best of them. Death holds no fears for you, does it? Mr Everett, let me tell you something. This makes *me* sick, and it ought to make you sick too. Look.'

Emerson takes young Mr Everett's head between his hands and points it at all that remains of Andrew Dryer. 'Look there! That's the enemy. The enemy won. Mr Dryer was fifty-six years old. I want you, Mr Everett – I want all of you –

to feel sick when you look at a body that has not reached its allotted three score years and ten. That is if you want to be doctors, not just money-grubbers.'

With this Emerson lets Everett have his head back, pushes his way through the remaining students, and stalks out of the room. As he gets beyond the students' hearing he says with some passion:

'Shit!'

The students remain uncorrupted by this expletive, but Mary Jo, on her way to Ken's room with a coffee, is deeply shocked by hearing such a word on the lips of so eminent a man. She blushes for him as much as for herself. She pauses for a moment before going in to face Ken. She tells herself that it is ridiculous to be sexually nervous of a man who has lost the use of his limbs, but nervous she is.

'Hello, hello, hello,' says Ken, taunting her as usual, and enjoying her discomfiture. 'Is that something to put into my face?'

'It's coffee,' says Mary Jo.

'No, it's not.'

'Yes, it is.'

'No, it's not.'

Mary Jo is nonplussed. Of course it is coffee; what must she say to convince him?

'It is, Mr Harrison, honest.'

'Joey, you can't shit a shitter.' (Again that word!) 'It's coffee-flavoured milk.'

Mary Jo laughs now the joke is over. It was harmless enough. She brings the paper cup to him: 'Come on, while it's nice and hot.'

'Jesus,' says Ken looking at it, for its appearance is even worse than usual. 'It looks sicker than I am. Just pour it in the sink and look innocent.'

'Come on, now,' Mary Jo insists. All her training has led her to the belief that no patient ever knows what is best for her or him. She is to have a rude awakening.

'No,' says Ken, quite sharply, and turns his head away, bumping her hand. The coffee is spilled onto the sheets, covering one shoulder, and half one side of his white gown. There is steam. Am I being scalded, Ken wonders. Seeing Mary Jo's shocked expression, Ken says, 'God, I'm sorry. What a dumb thing to do.'

'Honestly it's okay, don't worry . . .' She mops at the sheet with a towel. This has no noticeable effect on the sheet, but turns the towel brown. 'We'll just have to change the sheets . . .' But it's not just the sheets which are stained; the gown and the pillows are also brown.

Mary Jo is keen to get the evidence of the accident obliterated before Rodriguez discovers it. She removes the pillows from under Ken's arms, sits him up and mops anxiously with her towel at the base of his spine. As she does so, she is unwittingly tugging at the middle half-sheet. Ken lurches away from her. As he starts to fall head-first over the edge of the bed, he yells out:

'Joey! Joey!'

Mary Jo launches herself across the bed, grabbing at his thigh, at his hip, at his gown. Ken's fall is arrested, but he is dangling upside-down, his head no more than a few inches from the ground, nor has Mary Jo the strength to pull him back onto the bed. When she tries, he slips from her grasp again.

'Christ! Joey ...' cries Ken, but Mary Jo is already calling for someone to come and help her, and she has not long to wait. Rodriguez appears with a male orderly. Then Dr Scott with another nurse. They hold Ken steady while the nurse strips the bed and changes the sheets. Scott puts a comforting arm around him, then realises that he will be unable to feel it. His eyes engage hers for a moment. There is a look of such bleak despair at his helplessness in Ken's eyes that Scott has to turn away.

Meanwhile Rodriguez is trying to get Mary Jo to help, but the unfortunate girl cannot move. 'Snap out of it!' Rodriguez cries.

As sardonic as ever, Ken says: 'I've been waiting to see who lived under the bed.' To protect Mary Jo from the wrath of Rodriguez (a fate worse than death it would seem) Ken claims responsibility for the accident himself. 'It wasn't her fault,' he insists.

This inconvenient moment is the moment chosen by Emerson, continuing on his rounds with his group of chastened students, to come into Ken's room. It takes much to startle Emerson, but he is taken aback by what he sees. In the arms of Rodriguez and Scott and in his stained gown, Ken is humiliated and yells:

'Get those jokers out of here. This isn't a circus.' But the students keep coming. 'Out! Out!' cries Ken. 'They are just changing the sheets. Medically speaking, this is not enlightening! The stains on my gown come from pure unblended Brazilian coffee grains and my hair is styled by Réné of Paris. Now out!'

Emerson glances at Scott who gives a scarcely

perceptible nod. Emerson motions for the students to leave, which they do, sheepishly. As Ken is lowered into his freshly made bed, Emerson inquires: 'What happened?'

'Nothing,' says Ken in a loud voice.

'Then why are you so upset?'

Rodriguez shoos the orderly, the nurse and a reluctant Mary Jo out of the room, then explains:

'He almost fell out of bed, doctor.'

Emerson: 'Really? And how do you feel now, Harrison?'

'Oh, great, fantastic! It's dandy getting out of bed. I was thinking of taking in a movie and a pizza.'

'Let's take a look.'

Emerson feels Ken's arms, shoulders, trunk, with casual expertise, then asks Ken to turn his head gently from side to side. Evidently all is as it should be.

'You'll be fine,' says Emerson.

'Are you kidding?'

Looking through the notes on the chart at the foot of Ken's bed, Emerson remarks that Dr Scott has increased the Valium dosage. Dr Scott admits that she has. But Emerson is well pleased with the patient's general condition, and the dialysis schedule is keeping him stable.

'What do you conclude, doctor?' Ken, feeling excluded and a little resentful, asks. 'Will I go down as one of your most notable successes?'

'You're doing fine. If we can manage to keep you in bed ...'

'*We*? And when do *we* get discharged?' Emerson smiles briskly, the smile of a television sports commentator, more cheering to the smiler than the smiled-at.

'You'll certainly be leaving here soon, I expect.'

'Discharged or transferred?'

'This unit is for critically ill patients, Mr Harrison, which, I am happy to say, you no longer are. You will shortly be moved to a rehab., which I'm confident you'll find a much more comfortable place.'

'Got it! You only grow the vegetables here. They're stored somewhere else.'

Emerson is no longer smiling. 'I don't think you understand.'

'On the contrary, I think I do. What would you say my chances are of being only partly dependant on nursing?'

'That's impossible to say with certainty at this stage.'

Ken looks directly at the doctor, unblinking.

'I am not asking for a guarantee, Doctor Emerson. I am simply asking for your opinion. Do you think I will ever walk again?'

Doctor Emerson remembers the time he had to tell a boy of fourteen that he had cancer, a raped girl that she would never be able to have a baby, a mother that her only son had died under anaesthetic, a model that she would have to have a breast removed.

'No, Mr Harrison, I don't think you will.'

Ken's voice is steady as he continues: 'Or regain the use of my arms? Or my hands?' Ken's hands lie, palm down, on top of the sheets. They are pale with prominent veins. The nails are uncharacteristically clean. Ken hardly recognises them as his own hands.

'No,' says Emerson.

Ken glances at Scott, who is smiling at him, then back to Emerson.

'Why didn't you tell me this before?'

'We were waiting for you to ask.'

'I see. Thank you.'

'For what?'

'Your honesty.' Ken's voice remains quiet, calm.

'Yes, well ... I know it's difficult, but it's better not to brood on it. It's surprising how we can come to accept things.'

'Good, you mean like falling out of bed?'

'Dr Scott has prescribed something which might help.'

'Terrific.'

Emerson turns to Dr Scott. He is relieved to have an excuse for breaking away from the patient's unblinking stare. 'You might get Mrs Boyle along.'

'Great idea,' says Ken, still calm.

'Goodbye, Mr Harrison. I'll look in on you later.'

'Better phone first to make sure I'm in.'

'Goodbye, Ken,' says Dr Scott, and both of them leave.

In the corridor Emerson's manner changes. He becomes matter-of-fact, decisive, one professional to another.

'Good, let's have him moved in a month, tops. All right, I'm off to a board meeting. Have to try to explain to those retards about inflation.'

'Have fun,' says Scott, putting a friendly hand on his arm.

'I'd rather have my prostate examined.'

*   *   *

It is then that Ken's loneliness overwhelms him, and he thinks of his father. He misses him. Is it possible to miss somebody you hate? Evidently it is. He had learned to hate his father on the day when his father, inflamed by bourbon, which he drank from a chipped mug with Donald Duck on the side of it, said that he hated Pat. Why did his father hate Pat? Because he leched for her. Because the stupid man leched for every girl Ken had ever brought home with him. Because the drunken creature was jealous of Ken's youth and vigour.

Remove the cause, and the effect should wither. Would Ken's father hate him now? Would Ken be able to forgive him? He had asked Pat about it. Pat had said it was very simple. Pat had explained that, Ken's mother having died when Ken was born – through the clumsiness of an inexperienced doctor, Ken believed, though there was no way of proving anything – Ken's father had not only lost his regular bed companion, but his cherished independence. He had been a traveller in novelties. Humorous bathroom fittings, chicken-skin fans painted (in Quebec) with saucy scenes of fin de siècle debauchery, chromium-plated cute executive toys for middle management, it was a living. More than that, it enabled him to express himself, which he did most creatively with a bottle at one end and a whore at the other. After Ken's birth, all that had to stop. He had to work from home, from

33

Boston, where he could get bottles in, but not whores. He lost his appeal to women; maybe he felt that Ken stole it from him. Certainly it was true that when girls began feeling weak at the knees for Ken, women began feeling strong-minded where Ken's father was concerned. When Ken's father met Pat it had been a disaster. Pat carried sensuality around with her like a shopping bag. Not her fault, but something she had been born with, made more potent by her dancer's training. Ken's father was not to know this. He assumed she was hot for him. He had also been at Donald Duck.

That had been it, so far as Ken was concerned. He had moved out at once, taking only what he could carry, and into Pat's place; later to a studio large enough for Ken to paint and sculpt, and for Pat to stretch her supple limbs and leap around. What had become of his father? Ken often wondered. Had the independence he had desired so fervently and for so long come too late? Did Donald Duck console him to the exclusion of all other interests? Or did he remove from the attic and dust down the cases of humorous bathroom fittings, the chests of chicken-skin fans, the (probably by now rather corroded) cute, middle-management executive toys?

So now, against all the odds, Ken longs to see the half-shaven grizzled chin, the stubble-hair, the red-rimmed, calculating eyes, and to tell his father that he, Ken, is close to despair.

Dr Scott breezes in, carrying all before her, including Valium.

'Hi!' cries Ken, falsely cheery, thrusting the panic back down out of sight, where it belongs. 'I

34

was just practising lying here. What can that impressive-looking pill signify? Has the hospital decided that I am a poor investment after all? Is this The Way Out?'

'Just something to help you relax.'

'From the fall? I'm just angry. But I'm all right.'

'We'll change the nurse. She's not experienced enough.'

'Don't do that. It was just an accident. It wasn't her fault. At least I have someone around here I can talk to.'

'Okay. I'll have a word with Miss Rodriguez.'

'It's just that I'm so damned helpless. I lie here like a fat blob.'

Dr Scott brings him the pill in a cardboard cup, and another cup of water. Ken turns his head away, protesting violently, but Dr Scott persists. Much irritated, Ken cries out: 'For Christ's sake, don't give me that, okay?'

'It'll make you feel better.'

'Quieter, you mean, and that will make you feel better.'

'Dr Emerson and I are in full agreement that you need this.'

'Why? Because I'm excited? Frustrated? Angry? Listen, if I want to be mad, I'll be mad. If I want to make a noise, I'll make a noise! Just because you're disturbed, because you can't do anything for me doesn't mean that I'm the one who gets tranquillised.'

'It is prescribed.'

'You haven't heard a word I've said. All I've got left is my consciousness. I don't need it paralysed as well. Understand?'

'Ken, I hear what you're saying.'

'Well, that's something. Now, if you want tranquillity, *you* eat the pill.'

Sighing, the handsome Dr Scott puts the pill back into its cup, where she rattles it rather forlornly. 'Well, you're not due till noon. We'll see then.'

'That's what I always say. If you don't know whether to take a tranquilliser or not, sleep on it.'

* * *

Air and light and space.

He had made it from his father's house to the airy, light and spacious studio he had shared with Pat, and then he had made it to this ... *vegetable patch*.

So they say he will never walk again; not walk, that's bad. If one can't walk how can one get to the tops of mountains, how can one get to swim in rivers, how can one get to those places where others do not go? An artist needs to be alone sometimes, needs to be away from other voices, needs to listen to the only voice that matters, uninterrupted. And they say he will never use his hands again; not use his hands – that's worse. If one cannot shape with one's palms, mould with one's fingers, one can create nothing, except dreams. Without solitude, without art, dreams could become obsessive, driving one's mind into the regions of the damned. Maybe they realise that, and therefore want to drug him into unconsciousness. They always have a reason for doing what they do. In half a year he has learned that, if nothing else.

* * *

'You want my Jell-o?' Emerson asks Scott. There is plenty of air and light and space in the cafeteria. Beyond the wall of windows the sky is the colour of silver. Emerson and Scott have a table to themselves. Both wear their white coats.

'No thanks.'

'Good. It's the only edible thing on the tray.'

'Eccentric of you, in that case, to offer it to me, Michael.'

'About Harrison ...'

'He refuses to take the Valium.'

'Oh?'

'He says he's got nothing left except consciousness, and he wants to keep that clear.'

'That's the trouble with all this anti-drug propaganda,' Emerson says gruffly. 'It gets in the way of treatment.'

'Maybe he's right.' Dr Scott brushes her hair back from her head. Why, with so many patients to worry about, is she constantly nagged by Harrison?

'You believe so, Claire? When he came in, shocked to hell, did he protest the saline drip? Or when he was gasping for breath, did he refuse to take the solumedrol?'

'Those were inevitable and emergency decisions.'

'So is this one.'

'How does a depressant drug improve his

consciousness? I mean, he could just want to *think*, you know.'

'Look, Claire, we have to help him accept his condition. Then maybe his full consciousness will be useful to him, but not till then.'

'Maybe.'

'Right. We're in a maybe profession.'

Claire Scott begins to pile her dishes onto her tray. She is obviously upset. 'I always thought,' she says sharply, 'it was meant to be an art.'

As Claire stands, so does Michael Emerson. He is taller than her, and feels that he needs this authority.

'Ken Harrison is an intelligent, sensitive and articulate man. But that doesn't mean he can prescribe for himself. If you don't wish to treat your patient, I'll be happy to take him on.'

With this, Emerson crosses the cafeteria to a wall-phone and punches the numbers for an internal line.

'This is Dr Emerson. Please prepare Valium ten m.g. I.V. for Mr Harrison. I'll be right up. Thank you.'

Ken is astonished when Dr Emerson enters the room with syringe and sterile wipe at the ready. Does it matter so much to them to humiliate him? He will have to be very careful, very cool. His only chance is to persuade them that he really had no need of sedation, no really, he is fine now, it had been a shock, hearing the news, they would understand that.

'Oh – oh, they've sent in the godfather.' And maybe this flippant tone is a bad start too. Dr

Emerson does not look like the life and soul of the party, like a man who would enjoy a joke and a bottle with a chum.

'How goes it, Mr Harrison?' And without even waiting to learn 'how it goes', Emerson pulls back the bedclothes and reaches for Ken's arm. Ken concentrates on keeping his anger out of his voice as he says:

'Dr Emerson, don't stick that needle in my arm.'

'You don't even know what's in it,' says Emerson, not unlike a mother trying to persuade a child to take a spoonful of an unfamiliar dish.

'Probably one of the drugs you use to keep me alive.'

'That's right.'

'Then forget it. I've decided I don't want to stay alive.'

Emerson pauses a moment in his preparations. He looks into Ken's eyes: 'You can't decide that.'

'Why the hell not?'

Emerson rolls up Ken's sleeve. 'Because you're very depressed.'

In fact Ken feels a great deal less depressed than for some time past. 'Does that surprise you?'

'Of course not.' Emerson is swabbing Ken's arm with the pad. 'In time you'll accept your situation. Until then let us help you.'

It's as much Emerson's silky way of talking as what he is about to do that infuriates Ken. At the top of his voice he shouts:

'Don't stick that fucking thing in me!' Emerson

ignores him. Ken feels nothing as the needle slides home, he is not even aware that he has lost the battle as he cries out: 'God damn you!' But then he knows; from the scarcely noticeable smile on Emerson's lips he knows. With as much authority as he can muster, Ken announces: 'I refused you permission to do that.'

'It was necessary,' says Dr Emerson, and cranks the bed down to a horizontal position. 'Now try to sleep.'

Quietly, because he wants to conserve his energy, Ken says:

'I don't want to goddam sleep. I want to goddam think!'

Emerson puts a hand on Ken's wrist, and, as if from force of habit, feels for the pulse. 'When you were sculpting and your statue wasn't coming out right, did you quit?'

'No. Anyway, they never come out right.'

'Well, neither do I quit.'

'What am I to you?' Ken asks. 'A lump of clay?'

As Emerson straightens out Ken's sheets, he says: 'No. You, pal, are a valuable life.'

'Don't call me pal!'

Now they know each other for what they are, enemies. Ken knows that they will remain enemies until one of them is defeated. He has no very clear idea of what that defeat will mean, but he is quite determined that he will not be the one to submit.

Dr Emerson is angry when he leaves his tranquillised patient. He remains angry longer than Ken remains awake, and that is a small victory for Ken.

                    *   *   *

Pat is dancing for him. And she is light and she is
space and she is air. She is in filmy white and he
can see her body through the gauze. She spins and
turns and hovers and glides to the call of the sea-
gull. Her hair flows. His fingers ache to trace her
outline in the air. He is moulding her. There is
plastiline and there is wire. He has created her out
of the air.

But now she is in black leotards in the studio
and her hair is up. He is in his favourite chair and
she is dancing for herself and to her reflection in
the mirror. He has ceased to exist for her. She is
creating herself out of the air. And he is filling his
pad with images of her.

Later when she has danced all the mystery out
of herself, and he has sketched her until she is
complete within the pages of his pad, she comes
over to him and puts her hands around his face
and brings her lips to his. As they kiss he knows
only the warmth and softness of lips, the roughness of tongue, the hardness of teeth; and her
body . . .

Now she is dancing *him*. He is the dance. She is
naked and her eyes are wild. She is in a fog. Where
she goes the fog melts. She is in the dark. Where
her body is, light is created. She moulds him out of
the air. He shapes her with his hands. Nothing
exists except light. Nothing exists except Pat.
Nothing exists except –
    'What?'
    'Sorry. We don't want bedsores.'

'We also don't want to be awakened every two hours for the rest of our lives.'

'You'll get used to it.'

'No ...'

The nurse – one he hasn't seen before – leaves the room.

'No,' he repeats. No. He knew now. There was nothing they could do to him now. He had the air, the light, the space. It awaited him. All he had to do was reach out for it. Rather that than ...

He is in a Hoyer lift, supported by canvas while Rodriguez and Mary Jo replace his old mattress with a new one. They are helped by two orderlies. He is calm and cheerful and the sight of Rodriguez's rear end while she bends over his bed is the eighth wonder of the world. Light and air and space indeed.

'Rodriguez, from here I get a remarkable view of your finer parts.'

'Okay, Mr Harrison.'

'Okay what? Come on, Rodriguez, love may be blind, but lust just doesn't care.'

'I'm going to wash your mouth out with soap.'

'Watch it, I bite.' As the orderlies lower Ken back into his bed and detach him from the sling, Rodriguez says:

'You are an impossible man.'

Ken glances at Mary Jo, who grins and blushes and looks away.

'Make that improbable.' Ken continues in a more serious tone, as Rodriguez settles the sheets around him. 'Rodriguez, do you remember the lawyer who came here about the insurance a few months ago? His name was something Hill.'

42

'I remember him.'

'I'd like to see him. If I'm going to be just hanging out, I probably can use the money.'

'Good thinking in there.'

'His card is in my drawer. Call him for me?'

'No problem.'

As Rodriguez searches for the lawyer's card, Ken asks Mary Jo: 'Are you qualified to scratch noses?'

'Sure.'

'You wanna give this one a try on the right side?'

As Mary Jo leans over Ken, her breasts are brought close to Ken's face. He can smell the starch. He can read the name on the I.D. ticket, and appreciate how little justice the tiny photograph does to Mary Jo's agreeable features.

'A little lower. Ah, that's the place. Good. Now higher. Now, would you scratch my ear?'

As the obedient girl does, her breasts touch his cheek.

'Oh, thank God for small mercies. Just chase it around. It keeps moving, you see. Beautiful. *Fantastic.*'

Rodriguez feels that the time has come to interrupt.

'Right, here it is, Mr Harrison. Carter Hill.'

'Right. Carter. I appreciate it. Thank you, both of you.'

Ken has hopes of Carter Hill. It is a hopeful sort of name. Agricultural but determined. A lot will depend on Carter Hill. A lot will depend too on Pat. He dreads her visit as he has never dreaded it before.

She looks more beautiful than ever, as if she has

43

guessed at his intentions, as if she has been refined by the pain. But how could she have guessed? He can hardly bear to look at her. He is dazzled. But when she comes to the bedside and bends to kiss him he turns his head smartly to one side so that her mouth brushes only his cheek.

'How are you today?' Pat asks, a little puzzled.

'Fine.'

'You don't seem the same, Ken.'

'You know you come here every day. That's really remarkable.'

'What's so remarkable about it? I love you.'

'I know. I feel honoured by that, and moved.'

Pat sits on the bed and looks closely at her man. She is used to his moods by now, and reckons she can handle them, but this doesn't seem like a mood. Whatever it is, she decides that she doesn't care for it at all.

'What's wrong with you today?'

'Pat, let me ask you a question. We make little jokes about cute nurses. Hints of sex. Obviously I haven't slept with anyone for over five months, but have you?'

'No.'

'Why not?'

'Because I'm not interested in other men. I love you.'

'Listen, without being self-pitying, I'm no longer someone to love. What I am now is an object who has to be taken care of for the rest of its life.'

Pat takes hold of his hand. Maybe he can't feel the gesture, but he can see it. He sees it, but can neither squeeze her hand, nor pull his away in response.

'I'm on a kidney-machine for four hours every other day. It's supposed to keep me "stable".'

'I knew that. It doesn't matter to me.'

'But it matters to *me*. I know you love me, Pat, and when I was Ken Harrison I loved you. But that was a long time ago. That was twenty-five weeks and a spine ago. I am no longer the man who loved you, Pat, nor the man whom you loved. You've been loyal, self-sacrificing . . . and I no longer want it.'

'What do you want?' Pat asks in a mild voice. She still has hold of his hand.

'I want you to walk out of this room, out of this hospital and never come back.'

'I'm going to put it down to your waking up in a bad mood, and –'

'You think I got out of bed the wrong side? Chance would be a fine thing! No, it's not that. I want you to find a man, Pat, get married, have babies.'

Bitterly Pat says: 'What am I supposed to do, go to the Salvation Army?'

'Listen, if you were lying here and I was sitting on the bed holding your useless hand, I would leave you.'

'When you are at your most selfish, you are very entertaining, Ken.'

'I'd leave you. I'd love you, but I'd leave you.'

Now Pat is really angry. She stands up and shouts at him, her arms rigid by her sides, her cheeks flushed.

'Oh, you would, would you? Well, you've got a lot of balls to lie there and make decisions about what we're going to do with our future. Of course I know it's going to be a lot different from anything we

45

thought it would be, but it's still *our* future. Half of it is mine. And everything we've ever been to each other, or done for each other, or taught each other is part of me now. I won't give it back because I can't give it back.'

'Don't you understand,' says Ken, and he has difficulty getting the words out because of the lump in his throat, 'don't you understand that every time you walk into this room, you remind me of what I can't do, and will never do again, and I can't take that. I know you love me. If you don't want to nurse me, you'll go now ... Please, Pat, *please*.'

'Ken, could I just say – '

'No, you can't! Don't you understand? I don't ever want to see you again. It's too much for me, too much.'

Because she does understand Pat nods and bends over him to kiss him goodbye.

'Don't,' says Ken, and again turns his face away from her kiss.

She looks at him for a moment, and once more he turns his face on the pillow. Then shuts his eyes. Sobbing at last, Pat reaches for her bag, knocking over the straggly chrysanthemums she had brought for him the previous day, and rushes out of the room. John sees her go.

Courageously John enters Ken's room and, glad to be of use, picks up the flowers and stuffs them back into the vase. Then he notices the tears on Ken's cheeks.

'I always say that a man can't use his arms, he's gotta be a real dumb sonofabitch to cry. I mean, it's just a way of getting your gown wet, man.' He takes a wad of tissues from the bedside cabinet and dries Ken's eyes and cheeks with them.

'Thanks, John, I'll be all right.'

Mumbling a bit, John says as he goes, 'Didn't do nothing except save myself the trouble of carrying a wet gown all the way to the laundry.'

PART 2
SITTING DUCK

The hospital is very proud of Ken. They have high hopes of him when they get him to the therapy class. No doubt they feel that to have a professional artist and sculptor there will encourage the other patients to weave more beautiful baskets.

John tells him this, amongst other things, while easing him into the specially adapted and specially expensive wheelchair. Ken realises why he is so cheered in John's presence. John alone of the entire hospital staff can see the absurdity of mankind's existence on this planet in general and of Ken Harrison's existence on this planet in particular.

'It is a joke, man, this whole place. One floor, people dying from poisoned air and water. Next floor, women having belly tucks. To keep you alive they spend thousands of dollars a week. In Africa children die of the measles when it would only cost a few bucks to keep them alive. *And* powdered milk for babies! Man, there's something crazy somewhere ... Listen, Ken, you free tonight? You wanna come hear my band play? I asked that Mary Jo, but it was working on an anatomy final. I told it that I was an expert on anatomy, and would be very happy to show it the hard bits! Then Rodriguez got after me, which is *big* trouble.'

'So who's my blind date?' Ken asks as soon as he can get a word in.

'A real nice lady.'

'The next thing you're going to tell me is that she's lots of fun.'

'It's Mrs Boyle.'

John pushes Ken at a great rate down the hospital corridors, taking the curves on one wheel. Accelerate out of them is the trick apparently.

'Mrs Boyle is therapeutics, isn't she?'

'Sure is.'

'Oh, Jesus, do I have to see her?'

'Dr Emerson's instructions.'

'Well then, I'd better. He's quite capable of dissolving her in water and injecting her into me.'

The Solarium is the best room in the hospital. It has a glass roof, new furniture, plants in pots. There is air, light and space. Unfortunately there are also people, and these people are neither as new nor as tasteful as their surroundings. Some talk reluctantly to relatives. A few talk to each other. One or two talk to themselves. An elderly man in a bathrobe which looks as if it has come straight from the costume department of MGM is playing solitaire, cheating, yet still losing. Mrs Boyle is there too, waiting for Ken. She is about thirty-five and wears a brown frock, a little too long to be chic. Otherwise most would think that 'she'll do'. Ken doubts it. John pushes him over to her and tweaks his cheek.

'Mr Harrison?' The voice is passionate with optimism.

'I used to be.'

'My name is Mrs Boyle.'

'And you're here to cheer me up.'

'I wouldn't quite phrase it like that.'

Mrs Boyle suggests that John push Ken over to

a particularly optimistic corner of the room. They pass the solitaire player.

'How's it going, Ken?' the old man asks. Ken wonders why he should be so familiar on such a brief acquaintanceship.

'Oh great! This charming lady is here to cheer me up. Stick around. She may perform a belly dance or saw me in half or something.'

The old man thinks Ken means it. His eyes light up.

'Not exactly,' smiles Mrs Boyle, the professional kill-joy. When they reach the corner upon which she has set her heart, she instructs John to apply the brakes to the wheelchair and leave them *à deux* for a *tête à tête*. Mrs Boyle had spent her previous summer vacation in Paris. Then she takes a deep breath, puts on a *special* smile of love and condescension.

'I've come to see if I can help.'

'Yes, you can.'

'How?'

'Go and convince your colleague, Dr Frankenstein, that he has successfully made his monster and can let it go. It promises to harm no one.'

'I'm told you don't want any more treatment.' (The ultimate heresy, thinks Mrs Boyle.)

'Good.'

'Why good?'

'Because I didn't think anyone around here heard me.'

'I heard you, Ken, loud and clear, and I want to know – I *need* to know – why you don't want any more treatment.'

'Because I don't want to go on living like this.'

'Why not?'

53

'Isn't that obvious?'

'Not to me, it isn't. It's a lousy break but you'll be surprised at all the things you'll be able to do with training and a little patience.'

'Such as?'

'You'll be able to operate a reading machine. And quite possibly an adapted typewriter. Maybe even a calculator.'

'Gee! And wow! The three Rs. But that does not of itself make for a full and abundant life, would you say?'

Mrs Boyle starts to light a small, black cigarette, recalls where she is, and stubs it out nervously. She fiddles with her wedding ring. What should *that* tell me, Ken wonders.

'You were a sculptor before your accident, and taught at the university?'

'I was a sculptor, yes,' Ken sounds defensive. He wonders where this line of argument is likely to take him.

'Don't you realise that you can still teach? Mr Harrison, there are some C-5s and C-4s with your same disability on the staff of Boston University.'

'I only taught in order to sculpt. I did not sculpt in order to teach.'

'Okay. Monet was almost blind when he painted the water lilies. Renoir was so crippled they tied his brushes to his hands.'

'Of course Monet and Renoir might have done even better if they hadn't been blind and crippled.'

'Then there was –'

'Oh come on, Mrs Boyle. I am not an avid fan of the Readers Digest.'

At last Mrs Boyle, showing unmistakable signs of being affronted, stops smiling.

'I do beg your pardon, Mr Harrison. *Those* people do not deserve such a casual insult. I work with brain-damaged children who crawl – literally – miles on their hands and knees, just *trying* to have what you have, an agile and creative and very whole mind. I can't stomach seeing you throw it away. Sculpting isn't the only art. Have you considered dictating into a tape recorder, writing a book on the plastic arts, or a novel? Poetry, perhaps?'

'You think you just change your art like switching your major in college? I was born a sculptor. My imagination – my whole being – speaks through my fingers. You people seem to think it's about survival no matter what. If I'd wanted to write a novel, I'd have written one. If I'd wanted to dictate poetry, I would have.'

Mrs Boyle is on the scent and baying. A dialogue has been engaged upon. Ken is 'wide open'.

'How do you know you couldn't do some of these things unless you try?'

'Because the trying isn't important. It's the work itself that's important, not completing it, not the rewards, not the credit, just the *work*. And the work is what I shall never do again.'

Mrs Boyle leans right forward and looks into Ken's eyes. She places a consolatory hand on Ken's knee. Intensely she says: 'But why not just *try?*'

'Jesus,' says Ken to himself, not to her.

'I know' – and now Mrs Boyle is brisk and positive again – 'let's make a start with the reading machine.'

'They have a lot of books for that machine?'

'Oh yes, many.'

'Fine. I'd like to make a request for my first choice.'

'Oh good. What's that?'

'"Sculpture With No Hands – Self Taught".'

'Why don't I come back tomorrow with the reading machine? Give it a chance, eh?'

'Jesus, it's marvellous. All you people are the goddam same! When I say something really awkward, you pretend I haven't said anything at all. Why can't you relate to patients as human beings, Mrs Boyle?'

'I'm sorry if I sounded detached.'

'Please. Just go ahead and detach yourself. Like right now.'

'I can understand your anger, Mr Harrison. In the circumstances it is perfectly natural –'

Stung beyond endurance, Ken shouts at the top of his voice. His frustration bounces off the new furniture, threatens to shrivel the potted plants, shatter the glass roof.

'Christ Almighty, you're doing it again. I say something insulting about you and you turn the professional cheek. If you were human, if you were treating me as a human being, you'd tell me to go screw myself. Can't you see that this is why I don't want to go on living? I'm not human any more, I'm even more convinced of that by your visit than I was before ... So how do you like that? The very exercise of your so-called professionalism makes me want to die.'

No sooner has Ken uttered these words than his lung muscles go into spasm and he can no longer breathe. This is something Mrs Boyle is not trained to deal with. Her patient says he wants to die, and at once sets about doing so. Mrs Boyle

56

panics and starts to stammer. Ken manages to produce a few strangulated words. Mrs Boyle listens carefully. They may be his dying message to humanity. They are:

'Go … for God's sake get out …'

'Nurse!' Mrs Boyle is humiliated as well as terrified.

'I … can't …'

'Nurse!'

' … breathe.'

'Oh God.'

John is first on the scene. He releases the brakes on the wheelchair.

'For Christ's sake,' Ken gasps, 'get me out of here.'

Mrs Boyle watches him go in a state of imminent nervous collapse. She had meant well. She had tried to be sympathetic. She had thought she *was* sympathetic. But the result is *this!*

'Oh God,' she whispers, long after Ken has been pushed away out of her range, 'Oh God, I'm so sorry.'

The journey back is hectic. Ken is gasping, perspiring, his head rolling from side to side.

'Relax, man, relax,' John suggests, taking the corners at full tilt. By the time they reach Ken's room, his face is blue. Rodriguez sees the crisis from the nurses' station, and is first off the mark; Mary Jo goes for Dr Scott. Rodriguez removes the oxygen mask from the wall, as John wheels the chair over to her. But as Rodriguez puts the mask to Ken's face, Ken twists and turns his head violently to avoid it. Rodriguez grabs his head and forces the mask over his mouth and nose.

'Stop fighting me, Mr Harrison.'

'Holy cow,' mutters John.

'Come on, now, that's it, breathe easily.'

'Man, I can't handle all this exercise,' says John.

Weakly through the mask Ken mutters: 'I thought all you guys were track stars.'

Rodriguez begins to cluck like a mother hen. She takes the mask off his face with many threats of wrath to come if Ken misbehaves. Then, with John and assorted volunteers from the nurses' station to help, she manoeuvres Ken from wheelchair to bed, a lengthy process.

Exhausted, Ken does his turn. In a faint voice he says to anyone who cares to listen:

'Hear the one about the secretary and her boss? She said, "I have good news and bad news. The good news is you're not sterile …"'

John laughs and says: 'The good news is that I called Mr Hill for you. He said he'd come by tomorrow but didn't know exactly when.'

'I'll be in all day.'

'Hi!' calls Doctor Scott from the doorway. 'What the hell *is* this, Grand Central Station?'

'Well, I've gotta catch a train,' says John, and leaves. The others melt away which, in Rodriguez's case, is a considerable feat. Doctor Scott sits on the bed; she sits on beds with some style.

'What was all the fuss about?' she asks Ken.

'I had a run-in with Mrs Boyle. She reckoned I had some kind of a future as a quadraplegic secretary-cum-chess-computer. I guess I should have smiled and listened and nodded and told her she was doing a grand job. The last thing I want is to bring Emerson down again with his pharmaceutical nightstick.'

'Well, I'm sorry about that.'

'It's not your fault. Is it?'

Dr Scott shook her head. 'Can I give you some advice? Take these pills; the dose is meagre. It won't dull your consciousness, not like the injection.'

'It's a deal.'

'Good. Here's one for now.'

'Okay.' Ken swallows it. 'But no social workers, check?'

'It's a deal.'

'You have beautiful breasts.'

Dr Scott blinks a couple of times in quick succession. 'I beg your pardon?'

'I said, you have beautiful breasts.'

'What an odd thing to say.'

'Why *odd*? I know you're a doctor, Doctor, but you must surely regard them as something more than mere mammary glands.'

'Well, of course, I –'

'You're perfectly safe, you know.'

'Of course.'

'I mean, I'm not about to leap out of bed and rape you or anything.'

'I know.'

'Do I embarrass you?'

'You surprise me.'

'And embarrass you?'

'Yes, I suppose.'

'Why exactly? I admit it's unusual for a man to compliment a woman on her breasts when only one of them is in bed. One of the people, I mean, not one of the breasts. But that's not the reason, is it?'

'Do you think it helps you to talk like this?'

'Because I can't do anything about it?'

'I didn't mean that exactly.'

'I've noticed you walking around this room, examining me, bending over my body, fixing your hair and it has amazed me to observe how relaxed a woman can become when she is not in the presence of a man.'

'I'm sorry if I've provoked you. I can assure you –'

'You haven't provoked me. But you are a woman and even though I've only got a piece of knotted string between my legs, I still have a man's mind. I spend my time engaging in sexual banter with the young nurses, just as I've been doing with you. Then they leave the room and I go cold with embarrassment. I disgust myself. Do I disgust you?'

'No.'

'Do you find me pathetic?'

'Sad. Just sad.'

There is a long silence. Doctor Scott thinks of the patient she has just come from, a brain tumour case, quite a young woman, her age. She must get back to her, but if she leaves Ken Harrison now, with a cheerful smile and a ready excuse, she will have no second chance with him. The Valium will begin to take effect soon enough; then she can go. She owes him another five minutes of her life. She will explain the situation later to the brain tumour, who will understand.

'I'm serious, you know,' Ken continues quietly. 'About wanting to die.'

'You'll get over that feeling.'

'How do you know?'

'Experience.'

'We all respond the same, huh? Like vegetables.

Plenty of feeding, plenty of watering, regular Valium ...'

'But if we acted on your decision now, you couldn't change your mind.'

'Yes, that's true.' Ken's voice is reflective, rather than bitter. 'I could become happy when a nurse comes to put in a new catheter or give me an enema or turn me over. Those could become the high points of my day. Those, and the drugs, of course. Or I might even surrender myself to Mrs Boyle and learn to do wonderful things like turning the pages of a book with my tongue or operating a typewriter with my eyelashes.'

'Would it be so terrible to have a free and working mind and plenty of time in which to put it to use?'

'Yes it would be, when that mind is only the computer section of a machine. And you would look at me and say: "Wasn't that worth waiting for?" And I'd be proud of my achievement ... Would you want me to be happy that way?'

'Ken, I don't think right now you know what you want.'

'Oh yes, Dr Scott, I do know what I want. My free and working mind keeps telling me what I want. And you have a moral obligation to accept my decision.'

'According to your morals. Not according to mine.'

'And why are yours better than mine? I'll tell you why. Because you are more powerful. I am in your power. Already I am beginning to get sleepy. It's the Valium you gave me. While I am asleep, there's nothing to stop you giving me something a little more powerful to ensure that, when I wake up, I don't give too much trouble, and take my next Valium like a good little boy.' Ken yawns. 'That yawn is why your morals are better than mine. But I warn you, Dr Scott, I shall cling on to mine with all the strength of a free and working mind.'

'I'll leave you now to have a rest. I was halfway through a patient when I was called away.'

As Doctor Scott reaches the door, Ken manages through another yawn to say: 'Oh, Doc.'

'Yes?'

'You do have great breasts.'

'Yes.' And Doctor Scott smiles.

'There now, that wasn't so hard, was it?'

* * *

Ken dreams of his schooldays. Names from the past, Randy Schumacher, Stan Noyes, Arnold O'Malley, John Du Pree, Wayne Jovanovitch, Wayne Wilson, Franklin Thomas, his gang. They had hunted in packs, terrorising the Boston suburbanites with their wild war-whoops, and strutting proudly, pigeon-chested in the sun. There had been girls then too, silly giggling creatures, who didn't know from nothing. None of them, not Randy nor Stan, not Arnold, nor Tom, nor either of the Waynes, nor Franklin, who had been his best friend, had visited him. Well it had all been many years ago, and they had drifted apart. One of his students had visited him, oh, maybe six weeks ago now. Billy Jacobson, tall, angular, a brilliant craftsman, but no innovator, had come with a pineapple. A *pineapple?*

'Didn't know whether you'd be allowed chocolates.'

(He would have been allowed chocolates, but not a pineapple. He did not tell Billy this, because Billy was as pleased as Punch to have brought something as unusual as a pineapple.)

'It's ripe enough, look.' And Billy had pulled at a leaf from the top of the pineapple, but the leaf had remained obstinately attached to its moorings. 'Well if it's not *quite* ripe today, you only have to leave it in the sun for a few days, and it'll be *amazing*.'

'Sure, Billy, but it's you I'm pleased to see. Really. Tell me all the news.'

Billy had told him all the news. There hadn't been much. Myra and Howard were splitting up finally, not that that was news exactly because they had talked about it for so long, but anyway they were, or said they were, and, after all, they ought to know. Billy guessed that was about it.

Myra and Howard were finally splitting up, and that was all that had been happening in his, Ken's, absence?

Well there had been talk of some kind of civic award for Ken in the light of all that he had done for the community. But Ken said he had no use for awards.

'Tell ya what,' Billy had said. 'We'll have such a party when you get out of this dump. Gee, I mean, it really will be a party, right? We've been talking about it a lot at the college, what a great party it'll be. We thought we might have it over at Myra and Howard's place.'

'I thought they were splitting up.'

'Oh well they are. I mean, like definitely, but

they haven't set a date. Not that you do set a date to split up, do you? I mean you set a date to get married.'

'Tell them I'll be out in 1990. You reckon they can stick each other's company that long?'

A gloomy silence had come between them. They could have been either side of the Berlin Wall. Billy had played unhappily with the pineapple, until it had toppled onto the floor.

'Thanks for coming, Billy,' Ken had said. 'It's been good seeing you.' Which had left Billy little choice but to go. And since then nobody. Only Pat. And now nobody. It was better that way.

But the following day Ken has a visitor, the one person in the world he *is* keen to see. John had wheeled him onto the terrace where a basketball match was in progress. Ken watches the sport with amazement. The play is vigorous and the wheelies dribble and pass, feint and shoot with the greatest facility. But, good as they may be, nothing can disguise the fact that it is an unnatural occupation.

'If God had meant paraplegics to play basketball,' Ken says aloud but to no one in particular, 'he would have made the goals bigger.'

Ken's visitor, Carter Hill, approaches at this moment. He's prematurely middle-aged and probably always will be. His head has grown through his hair in places. He reminds Ken at first sight of a well-groomed weasel. But Hill has seen Ken before. He works as lawyer for the insurance company, which has been handling Ken's case.

'Are you talking to me?' Hill asks. 'About God, I mean?'

'Oh, it's Mr Hill, isn't it? How are you?'

'Fine, thank you. Fine. You're looking a lot better than when I last saw you.'

'I'm as well as I'll ever be.'

There is a squeak of tyres on wood as the players undertake some delicate manoeuvres. Hill shakes his head in disbelief.

'Those guys are very good. Just like a real team.'

'Nah. Their dribbling sucks.'

A little disconcerted, Hill brings a chair over to Ken's wheelchair and, sitting down, immerses himself for a while in his briefcase.

'I've got all the papers here. Things should move very well.'

'I don't want to talk about the accident, Mr Hill.'

'Well, I can understand that, Mr Harrison, it's perfectly natural in the circumstances, but I'm afraid ...'

'No, no, no, no.' Ken's voice becomes loud enough to distract the athletes who look at him for a moment, affronted. 'I didn't ask you to come about the insurance claim.'

'You didn't? But I was led to believe –'

'You don't work for the insurance company, do you? I mean, exlusively?'

'No. I have my own practice.'

'Then you could represent me independently?'

'Yes.'

'In that case, Mr Hill, I'd like you to get me out of here.'

'I'm not sure I understand what you mean.'

'Well, it's really very simple. I want to be discharged from this hospital.'

'To another hospital?'

'No, not to another hospital.'

'Well, I'm sure they won't keep you here longer than necessary.'

'You wouldn't think so, would you ...? You see, I can't exist outside the hospital. They have to keep me here to keep me alive, which will keep them alive. And they seem to be intent on doing just that. But I have decided that I do not want to go on living like this, not even like *that*' - with a nod in the direction of the basketball players, still charging around the terrace like so many Ben Hurs - 'and so would like to be discharged in order to die.'

'And you want me to represent you?'

Ken looks at the unimpressive figure of the insurance lawyer and senses something there which will not easily be deterred from its set purpose, is reassured by what he sees, and manages a smile: 'Tough luck.'

'What an astonishing request,' says Carter Hill, and then, with mounting amazement, repeats himself.

'My sculpture isn't very orthodox either.'

'You mean just lie around somewhere and die?' Ken nods. 'And what is the hospital's attitude?'

'They don't know about it yet.'

Hill gets up from his seat and paces up and down, moving as though his shoes are a half a size too large for him.

'I don't know what to say, indeed I don't.'

'Look, Mr Hill. There's nothing left of me. I can do nothing for myself. Don't you think - you yourself - that I have the right to determine my own fate?'

'I don't know.'

Ken gives an angry bark of disapproval. He has

expected something better of Hill. 'Old prejudices die hard, don't they?'

But Hill is still wrestling with the problem: 'Yes, I suppose you do have the right. But you do realise –'

'Look, I'm not asking you to make any decision regarding my life. I'm just asking you to represent my position to the hospital. Now lawyers, in the name of Justice, represent criminals whom they know to be guilty –'

'I can't let *that* go, Mr Harrison. It's by no means as cut and dried as that ...'

'And they try to win for their clients, don't they?'

'Indeed they do.'

'Well then, can't I have the same rights as any axe murderer?'

Hill is not used to being on the receiving end of a cross-examination. He finds it a not entirely enjoyable experience.

'The first thing would be to see the doctor in charge.'

'Doctor Emerson.'

'Very well. I'll endeavour to see him now.'

'That means you'll represent me?'

'It means I don't know. Let me see Dr Emerson as a first resort.'

'But you will come back here and tell me your decision, even if Doctor Emerson convinces you that he is right?'

'I'll be back.'

Ken still has doubts about Carter Hill, but the weaselly fellow seems to sense this, for he leaves his briefcase on the lap-table of Ken's wheelchair as evidence of good faith.

'Thank you,' says Ken sincerely, adding in

better humour: 'And if anyone tries to steal it, I'll
swear horribly at them.'

        *   *   *

As an insurance lawyer Carter Hill is equally at
home in the world of the insurance office, the law
courts and the hospital. He has a separate style for
each. In the office he is bright and brisk, always
ready to share a doubtful joke with the boys, or
indulge in a mild flirtation with the girls; in the
courts he is deferential but tenacious, a difficult
man to get the better of in cross-examination; and
in the hospital he is sympathetic but deliberately
anonymous, a good listener. Little surprises him.
He prides himself on this, and he reckons that
when one moves between offices, hospitals and
courts there is very little that one does not know
about human behaviour. Perhaps for this reason
he has not married and scarcely expects to.

On this occasion however he has been very
much surprised by Ken Harrison, and is to be
surprised a second time in as many minutes when
he sees a black orderly wearing a colourful
bandeau wheeling a bandaged patient on a
gurney at a speed which would send most traffic
cops into convulsions. The orderly and his patient
arrive at an elevator just as the doors are closing.
Carter Hill would be less surprised if he could
have seen inside the elevator, as John had. For
within it is a young and attractive nurse with
curly hair.

'Made it,' gasps John. And to the patient: 'A
little extra ride. It'll make your day.'

68

'I'm going to Gynaecology,' says Mary Jo, as though that concludes the matter.

'Oh, he don't mind,' John says, and it's true because the patient appears to be unconscious.

Mary Jo pushes the appropriate button for Gynaecology. John seizes the opportunity.

'Why won't you go out with me? I've got a great collection of postage stamps. You really should see my unperforated Virgin Island Commemoratives.'

Mary Jo blushes as she was intended to. 'It's just that I can't ...'

'Negative thinking never got nobody nowhere.'

'I hardly know you.'

'Right. That's why we have to go out.'

The elevator has stopped and the doors start to open.

'Ask me next week after exams.'

'John.'

'John.'

'Okay. It's a deal.'

Mary Jo trots out of the elevator, glancing behind her and smiling. As John presses the down button, he adds: 'And I'll ask you this afternoon as well.'

On the way down John remarks to the patient on the gurney: 'Now, wasn't that fun?'

But to his astonishment a voice from within the bandages answers him: 'You're a fucking maniac!'

Meanwhile Carter Hill has been with Doctor Emerson, and it has not been a marriage of true minds.

'You know what you're asking?' says the doctor, who is furious, and beginning to show it. 'You're asking to kill my patient.'

'Doctor, I am simply presenting to you Mr Harrison's wishes in this matter.'

'And you do represent Mr Harrison in this matter?'

'Not yet. I told him I would have to talk to you before I made a decision.'

'All I can tell you, Mr Hill, is that releasing Mr Harrison to anywhere except a full-service hospital is tantamount to murder.'

'Murder is a legal term, Doctor Emerson. I'm only representing my client's needs and wishes *if* I choose to represent him.'

'You believe in capital punishment?'

'Oh come *on*, Doctor Emerson, let us at least –'

'Well, that's what you're recommending.'

'I'm not recommending anything. Yet.'

'Yet;' said Emerson.

There is a tap on the door of Emerson's office. A face appears round the door jamb. 'Would you like a cup of coffee, Doctor Emerson?' asks the nurse. 'And your friend?'

'No, we would not. Out!' And the face, aggrieved, vanishes from sight. Emerson continues:

'Look, Hill, we've spent over five months and one hundred thousand dollars of tax payers' money to save this man's life. We're not letting that go down the drain.'

'That is not the issue, with respect. What we should be discussing is a man's right to determine his own life, not the quality or expense of your treatment. Mr Harrison wants to be discharged from this hospital. Will you do that?'

'Like hell I will!'

'Why won't you?'

'Because it's my sworn duty to preserve life and

not to destroy it. And goddam it to hell, I'm not going to let that man die through some sort of legal chicanery.'

Now Hill is as angry as Emerson. They have never seen him like this in the office. He stands up and points a finger at his adversary.

'He *is* a voluntary patient here.'

'This interview is at an end, Mr Hill.'

'I may as well tell you that I can conceive of no legal constraints under which you may hold him against his will.'

'Just understand one thing: Mr Harrison is depressed at present, and incapable of making a rational decision about his own life, or death. And taking advantage of him in such circumstances is the lowest kind of venality.'

Hill feels some relief that Emerson has descended to personal abuse. An opponent who can do that is less likely to impress a judge, in Hill's experience. He is not tempted to reply in kind but merely asks:

'In your opinion then, Mr Harrison is mentally unbalanced?'

'He is.'

'Well in my opinion, Doctor Emerson, he is not.'

'Jesus Christ,' cries Emerson raising his eyes as though expecting an answer. 'You're not a doctor.'

'Would you object to my bringing in a properly qualified psychiatrist to examine Harrison?'

'We have several on our staff who would be happy to undertake such an examination.'

'I'm sure you'll understand if I ask for my own psychiatrist – whose opinion you will not be so sure of in advance.'

Emerson crosses to the door, opens it, and

stands to one side. 'Goodbye, Mr Hill.'

'Thank you for your time, Doctor.'

Emerson watches the lawyer go with distaste.
In the old days when he, Emerson, was qualifying,
a doctor was not saddled with all these lawyers,
bureaucrats, accountants, administrators, gov-
ernment inspectors. He could get on with the
business of saving people's lives. Now it was
becoming something of a luxury actually to get to
see a patient; indeed he often had the feeling that
things would run a great deal more smoothly if
there were no patients at all. Perhaps he should be
grateful to the patient Harrison for making his
gesture in that direction. Sighing, he picks up the
telephone.

'See if you can find Doctor Jacobs, Barbara, and
ask him to call me. And get me the Hospital
Administrator, would you?'

*   *   *

Ken is in therapy. He had been proud of his body
once. Of course it was Pat's stock-in-trade, so she
had to work out and diet and all the rest of it, but
for Ken it had become a pleasure to keep in shape.
He liked to think that if it came to the crunch he
could run the 100 faster, jump higher, lift the
weights with less difficulty than most of his
students, though that wasn't saying much, for
they were a liverish, beer-swilling lot. So now in
therapy it is not the pain which distresses him, nor
his failure to achieve the simplest of tasks (though
that would be distressing enough), but the sight of
his flaccid muscles and heavy thighs, all that

flesh, now quite superfluous to his needs.

The therapist is generous in praise of Ken, when he manages to develop his neck muscles in a series of basic exercises, but, since the episode with Mrs Boyle, Ken regards the praise of such people as meaningless. Carter Hill trots up to him in the Physical Therapy room, but Ken suggests that such information as Hill may have acquired should not be passed to him, Ken, publicly. Michael, the tactful masseur, takes the hint and retreats into his mystical world of liniments and embrocations, having put Ken back into his wheelchair.

'You see,' says Ken, directing Hill's attention to a safety strap holding him in place in his chair, 'I've taken to wearing a girdle.'

'On you,' says Hill, 'it's becoming.'

'A guy is putting on a girdle in the locker room after tennis. So his buddy asks: "Since when are you wearing a girdle?" "Since my wife found it in my car".'

Hill makes a brave attempt at a laugh. It's not that he finds the joke unfunny – he doesn't – but that he has spent too long listening to judges' witticisms and attorneys' laboured jests to be able to react spontaneously when jokes are told to him at parties.

As soon as the therapist and his various intended and prostrated victims are out of earshot, Carter Hill reports on his mission:

'Emerson does not want to discharge you.'

'So what else is new?'

'Mr Harrison, it's best that I should be perfectly straight with you. Emerson claims that you are not in a healthy enough mental state to make a rational decision, especially one as serious and final as this one would be. Now my problem is that I am not competent to judge whether or not he is right.'

'What will help you decide?'

'I would like to have you examined by an independent psychiatrist and I will accept his view of the case.'

'Fair enough, but will Emerson agree?'

'He already has.'

'Good work. That's a beginning.'

'He'll probably have the hospital psychiatrist examine you too, and I imagine we'll end up with conflicting views.'

'And where will that lead us?'

'Hard to say. Emerson was quite adamant about the whole thing. Wouldn't put it past him to try to use the Mental Health Law. That means that if he can get two psychiatrists to sign statements to the effect that you're mentally unbalanced, he can commit you here and give you any treatment he wants.'

'My God. He can really do that?' Hill nods. 'And I have no say in it?'

'Well, you can request a hearing and see how things go from there.'

Ken feels most tremendously tired. He feels that he will never be able to take any decision on his own again. The idea of testifying in front of a hearing panics him. He feels as though his paralysis is affecting his brain. Gloomily he mutters: 'Well, whatever, let's get on with it. Wheel in your shrink.' Then in alarm he looks Hill straight in the face and in his eyes Hill can see a pleading, pathetic expression quite uncharacteristic of the man. 'You will represent me?'

Hill rises, takes his briefcase from the lap-table of the wheelchair, and says: 'I don't know, Mr Harrison. Let's get the shrink in here first. I'll be in touch.'

'It's a fight for the death, right?' Ken is almost smiling.

'Right.'

PART 3
A FIGHT FOR THE DEATH

Sometimes when Dr Emerson sits at the desk in his office and looks at the bank of TV monitor screens, he feels like God. He realises the folly of such a reaction, and how inaccurately it reflects the reality of the situation, but, nevertheless, that is how he feels: inaccurate because he can only partly affect the lives of those patients in his charge. He can pump them full of drugs and steroids, he can cut out the cancers and anaesthetise the pain, he can keep them fed and washed and comfortable, but that is almost all he can do. Patients who seem to be convalescing suddenly suffer a paralysing attack; patients who seem to be dying suddenly sit up and ask for a hamburger; such occasions serve to remind him that his powers of diagnosis and of treatment are finite and that, despite his bank of TV monitor screens, he is as human as any one of his patients, and will himself inevitably succumb.

At any time of the day or night Emerson can flick a switch and study any of the Intensive Care patients and a few other favoured cases such as Ken Harrison. Constant read-outs reporting on their vital functions are presented to him, and not one of the patients may so much as blink without Emerson having notice of the function and the complicated reflexes therefrom.

When Dr Jacobs knocks and enters, Emerson is watching Rodriguez manipulating Ken's arms and listening to Ken's off-colour jokes at her expense. With Jacobs' entrance, he turns down the volume of Harrison's monitor.

'Dr Jacobs. Good of you to spare me the time.'

'Never too busy.' In fact Jacobs, a worried-looking man with horn-rimmed glasses, a dimpled chin and, surprisingly, a large sensual mouth, is always too busy, and knows it. A busy psychiatrist is little use to his patients. Emerson offers Jacobs coffee from a flask but Jacobs, easing himself into a chair, refuses. Coffee, he insists, keeps his heartburn awake.

'Who's your problem?'

'Ken Harrison. Thirty-two year old man, auto accident, severe trauma, cervical 4, transect, nephrectomy, dialysis, usual C4 complications. There he is.' Jacobs moves round the desk to see what the problem looks like.

'So?'

'He wants to be discharged, to discontinue dialysis, to go home and die.'

'Presumably he would?'

'Wouldn't last a week. I've about got him back, gave him steroids, balanced his electrolytes, stabilised the dialysis, and, lo and behold, we just about have a viable human being again.'

There is a knock on the door, and Doctor Scott comes in. Jacobs leaps to his feet, but Emerson stays put and does the introductions.

'I was telling Dr Jacobs about Harrison, Claire. He has gotten himself a lawyer and threatens to sue if we don't discharge him. Seems if I'm to keep him alive, we'll have to commit him under Mental Health.'

'I'll go talk to him,' says Jacobs, 'but even if I

agree that he is mentally incapable, you'll need another consult.'

'Is that a problem?'

'It depends if he's clinically depressed. If we walk in and he says, "Hello, I'm a teapot," you're in.'

'And he's in,' says Scott quietly. Emerson ignores this. 'Depressed? He's suicidal.'

Jacobs manages a humourless smile which many of his colleagues might take as symptomatic of nervous disorder and says:

'I could name you several psychiatrists who would not accept suicide as evidence of insanity.'

'I'll accept that. Okay. I'll talk to your suicide for you.' After all Jacobs is a professional.

'Good; thank you. And do me another favour, would you? For the second signature try to find an old bastard like me who believes in something better than suicide.'

Moving to the door, Jacobs says: 'I know an old bastard at St Josephs, a staunch Catholic.'

'Sounds perfect. I appreciate it, Sandy. And so, I'm sure will Harrison when he realises ...'

'Right,' says Jacobs, and goes.

'Right?' Emerson asks Scott. Evidently not, to judge by Scott's voice when she says:

'So we commit Ken Harrison as mentally incompetent.'

'He'll be dead within a week if we don't.'

'It's his life, Michael.'

'But goddam it, it's our responsibility. What has got into you? I thought you were with us on this.'

'I don't know who I'm with.'

'Look, Claire, I refuse to accept the fact that a

81

man of Harrison's intelligence would choose suicide.'

'But he has!'

'Therefore I say he's unbalanced.'

'That doesn't follow at all. It's like the old test for witches. You threw them into a river and if they floated that meant they were witches; if they drowned, then they were innocent.'

'We're not talking about witches, and this is the twentieth century.'

'Exactly. Look, who in hell owns Ken's mind and body? Do you? No. He does. Very well then, I believe it's his right to use them or dispose of them any way he sees fit.'

'Don't give me that "right to die" routine. We're committed to life. Look, when a patient is brought in here in his condition, I don't stand around wondering whether his life will be worthwhile. I haven't got time for that. I try to save it. I'm a physician, not a metaphysician, nor a judge.'

'Right now you're behaving like a judge.'

Claire is furious. As she is about to leave the room, Emerson realises that there is something else he ought to say to her.

'Claire, it may not be necessary to say this, indeed I very much hope that it isn't, but if Harrison should suddenly go sour and die on us, I'll order an autopsy and act on whatever's found. You know what I'm talking about.'

In Claire Scott's eyes there is a stubborn look which does not bode well for Emerson's peace of mind. She strides out on healthily determined legs. Left alone Michael Emerson turns his attention to the monitor screen relating to Harrison's room. John is loading Ken onto a gurney.

He is remarkably gentle, though to little purpose, since Ken can feel nothing of the strong black hands on his debilitated body.

'To dialysis?' Ken asks. John nods. 'How about a singles bar or a disco and skip the dialysis? What's this obsession with kidneys?'

'Uh uh.' John shakes his head. 'No dice. I need this job. It pays for the xylophone.'

'As the man about to be hanged said: "I'd just as soon skip the whole thing".'

'Not up to you, man. You know the hospital rules; whatever isn't forbidden is required. That's rule number two ...'

They have reached the room in which the kidney machine is waiting greedily for them. John puts the brakes on the chair as Ken asks:

'What's number one?'

'Whatever it is, don't get any on you.' There is a moment in which John senses Ken's depression beneath the surface glitter of his conversation.

'Hell, man,' John continues almost desperately, 'come on, there's a whole lotta things you can do.'

'Like what?'

'Well, let's see ... You can move your head, right? So you could fit an aerial on your head and be a radar antenna. Don't require no special training for that.' Rotating his head, John makes a beeping sound.

'Sure, or I could be a babysitter. Kids are always getting into trouble so I can be always shaking my head. Like this. That should keep the little wretches in order.'

'No! I got it! You could be a tennis umpire.' And John moves his head from side to side, clicking his tongue.

'Great. Yeah and when I get good at that, I can move on to ping-pong.' Ken clicks his tongue and moves his head from side to side faster, looking more than a little demented. Releasing the brakes, John pushes him into the dialysis room.

Here there are several machines, and a technician is just uncoupling a young girl from one of them. She wears a flowered dressing-gown and the sort of slippers that people used to give one another at Christmas.

'Hi, kid,' says Ken, as the technician sets about hooking him up to the machine.

'Hi, old man.'

'You know something, Lissa? You are absolutely gorgeous. Got your hair cut since you were last here, didn't you?'

The girl, who is about ten years old, is totally self-possessed. 'I'm not gorgeous,' she says. 'I have a mirror.'

'So?'

'I'm not gorgeous.'

'Mirrors speak with forked tongue,' says Ken in a bad imitation of a bad actor playing a bad Indian in a bad picture. 'Harrison he speak heap big truth. Ugh.'

'Guess what?' asks Lissa.

'What?'

'I'm being cut down to once a week.'

'Ah, that's wonderful, Lissa. Soon it'll be every two weeks, and then none. Then they'll send you home and you'll go to school and get a degree in surveillance techniques and become President of the United States of America and get shot at and come back in here. Oh boy, have you got a life ahead of you.'

84

Lissa has been lifted off the bed by a tech and now she is helped into a wheelchair.

'You'll get better, Ken,' she says.

'Oh I am, I am. Next spring I'm signed to play shortstop for the Red Sox.'

'Fantastic.'

'Only trouble is, that's the day I'm down to play Borg in Vegas.'

'Tough cookie.'

'Ain't it though?'

'Bye, Ken. See ya.'

'Bye, kiddo.'

John takes hold of the handles of Lissa's wheelchair and joins in the game.

'All right if I drive you home, Lissa?'

'Sure thing, buster. But you ought to see my sister!'

As they pass through the swing doors Ken hears John say: 'You ever been to a disco?'

* * *

Ken is still in dialysis when Doctor Jacobs pays him a visit. There is a hum from the machine and Jacobs has to raise his voice to be heard above it.

'Mr Harrison?'

'The very same. Welcome to the body-shop.'

'I'm Sandy Jacobs.' He pulls up a chair.

'And you're a psychiatrist?'

'Does it show?'

'Wife to husband: "You must be drunk, your face is all blurred." ' Jacobs barks with laughter. 'Well, Dr Jacobs, are you for or against me? Oh, does that sound like paranoia?'

'You'd hardly expect me to make an instant diagnosis.'

'I've no other engagements, so take your time. Did Emerson send you?'

'I work here in the hospital.'

'Ah!'

Jacobs clears his throat. He takes a hand towel which the tech had tactfully placed over the shunt in Ken's arm and unfolds it. Then: 'Would you describe yourself as suffering from paranoia?'

'No.'

'What would you say paranoia was?'

'It depends on the person. Someone who thinks that what he wants is right and will brook no denial may be paranoid. If that person is a sculptor, for instance, then we would characterise the condition as paranoia. If however, he is a doctor, we would describe it as professionalism.'

During this Dr Jacobs has folded and unfolded the hand towel. Now he laughs again and asks: 'So you don't like doctors?'

'Do you like patients?'

'Some patients.'

'I like some doctors.'

'What's wrong with doctors then?'

'You want my diagnosis? Very well then. I don't think most doctors realise that there are people who can and who *want* to understand what's wrong with them, and who are quite capable of making decisions about their own bodies.'

'And there are plenty of people who can't. What they need is information.'

'A joke,' says Ken. 'A pregnant young woman asks the doctor what position she will have to lie in to give birth to the baby. "The same position you were in when you started it." "My God," she cries. "Do you mean I've got to drive around Central Park in a taxi for two hours with my feet dangling out the window?" '

Even the tech laughs at that.

Jacob says: 'My point exactly. Patients need sound medical knowledge before they can make the right decisions.'

'Sure, look at me, for example. I'm a sculptor. A flighty artist with no capability for understanding anything about my own body. It just so happens that I could probably hold my own with you in a competition on anatomy.'

Jacobs folds and unfolds the towel. 'It's been a long time since I did any anatomy.'

'Whereas I was teaching it right up to the time of the accident. So you see it wouldn't be fair, would it?'

'Okay, Harrison, your knowledge of anatomy may be excellent, but what's your neurology like? Or your dermatology, endocrinology, urology, and so on?'

'Lousy, all of them, though I'm working on my escapology. And insofar as they have a bearing on my case, I should be grateful to have all the relevant information so that I can make the right decision. But right or wrong, it would be *my* decision. Suppose you came to my studio to buy something. You looked at all my pieces and finally said: "I want the mother and child." and I said: "No, no, no. You don't know anything about sculpture. You are having the flamingo." You would think I was crazy. You probably do anyway.'

'We're not talking about a piece of sculpture, but about your life.'

'That's right. *My* life. Think about that, Dr Jacobs.'

Ken is suddenly quite tired, and lies back with his head against the rest. He feels he has no more he can usefully say to this implacable psychiatrist. He hopes that Jacobs will agree with him. However, as Ken leans his head back, Jacobs leans right forward, seeming to draw strength from the other's weakness. He says:

'Your obvious intelligence weakens your case. I'm not saying that life is going to be easy. But you have resources because of your intellect which other people lack. It would be a shame to waste them.'

'My God, that's your Catch 22. If you're clever and sane enough to put up a convincing case for suicide, it demonstrates that you ought not to die.'

Jacobs folds and unfolds the towel. Sick with the play-acting, Ken goes onto the attack.

'That's a nasty little tidiness compulsion you've got there.'

Jacobs smiles, and there is respect and admiration in the smile. He also puts the towel back, hastily folded, on the shunt. 'I was an only child,' he murmurs, then, as though afraid that he is letting Ken off the hook: 'But we are not here to discuss me. Have you any relations outside the hospital?'

'When this happened I was living with someone, a woman, a ballet-dancer, and she was beautiful ...'

*

'I was living with this ballet-dancer. Yes, we were happy enough. Looking back on it now, we were very happy indeed, happier than before - or since ...'

'Yes, at the time of the accident I was with this beautiful girl, a dancer. Not in the car with her, living with her, you understand ...'

The psychiatrists all find Ken's period of happiness before the accident of peculiar fascination. They cannot come to terms with happiness at all. Indeed it begins to seem to Ken that they regard his affair with Pat as clear evidence of his insanity. Or maybe they are just plain jealous. He has had enough of their prurient questions. He has had enough of Dr Barrows, big, bold, black, burly, who is interrogating him now.

'Does she visit you often?'

'She did. She was very good. She came every day, usually with flowers. Two weeks ago I told her I didn't want to see her again.'

'She must have been very upset.'

'Better than a lifetime of sacrifice.'

'What about your parents? Are they living?'

'I have a father - somewhere. My mother died. Which isn't bad considering birthdays. And Christmasses. And presents. After all, how many hats can I wear?'

'I should like to do some tests ...'

Ken sighs audibly. 'What tests? I can tell you right now my time in the hundred yards dash is lousy.'

'And I'd like to confer with Dr Emerson.'

'Confer! That's when two doctors get together to support each other's mistakes.'

'Why are you so angry, Mr Harrison?' The sun is pouring through the window, so Dr Barrows has had Mary Jo pull the Venetian blinds. Now the shadows of the slats across the doctor's face give him a jungle appearance which Ken finds disconcerting.

'Oh, no shit, doctor. Just put me down as being in the manic phase of a manic-depressive cycle.'

'You are very free with psychiatric jargon.'

'Not fair is it when the patients start reading the text books? Well in my case you can always say I'm an obsessive hypochondriac.'

'I certainly wouldn't do that ... Mr Harrison, your lawyer, Mr Hill, was the one who asked me to see you. If anything, I'm on your team.'

'Dr Barrows, after being questioned by four shrinks, I feel that I'm a football being kicked around by both teams, and it ain't restful!'

'I can understand that, but it is necessary to be impartially professional.'

'God, can't you see what a trap I'm in? How the hell could anyone prove that he's sane. Could you?'

'I'll come and see you again. When you feel less aggressive towards me.'

'No, don't come and see me again, because the more you and the others come the more you make me angry and frustrated and depressed.'

'I'm sorry if I upset you, Mr Harrison, truly I am.'

'Please just leave me alone.'

Claire Scott is very much confused. She respects
Emerson, whom she knows to be an excellent and
skilful doctor, and since she works under him in
the hospital, she is reluctant to break off
diplomatic relations with him over Ken. But she
respects Ken Harrison more, and the respect has
ripened into something akin to love. She thinks
that she has never met a braver man. She does
not want him to die, but she does not want him to
be humiliated any further. When she is with Ken,
she wants him to win; when she is away from him
she is desperate that he should survive. And now
Emerson has sent her on a mission of supreme
importance. It is her job 'to find something'
(Emerson's words) 'that will get Mr Harrison to
change his mind'.

But what? She scarcely knows him. Obviously
she must get to know him better and, with this in
mind, she determines to visit Ken's home. If she
succeeds Emerson will have been justified; if she
fails Ken will die.

Ken's studio is in an industrial sector of the
city. It's a loft on the top floors of a square
brownstone warehouse with the legend above the
entrance: 'SUPREME LIGHTING CO.' She has
no idea what to expect, and, despite having made
contact with Pat, feels that to invade Ken's past
without Ken's permission is to behave like an
intruder.

Pat has been brusque on the telephone, has
said that the key will be under the mat (which it
is) and that she will be along just as soon as she

can get away from her performance. Claire imagines how she must feel about it all. Remarkable that she could play ball at all.

Claire has no idea what she may find in the studio. 'There *must* be something', Michael Emerson had suggested, 'that will trigger him into wanting to live, something in his past, in his environment, in his work. He's too superior a man to let go,' and Claire had been very touched by his passionate concern for his antagonist.

So now as she pushes open the studio door – she is a little out of breath from climbing the five flights of stairs – she is apprehensive as to what she will find.

Air and light and space. The air and the light flood in from a skylight. The space, though filled with Ken's artefacts, is breathtaking. It is filled with Ken – and with Pat. Photographs of Pat abound – she is in jeans, she is in leotards, she is nude. One photograph, which is larger than life-size, displays her in mid-*jetée*: she seems lighter than air.

Here she is again, sculptured in bronze, naked and one of a pair. The other nude is that of a man, potently muscular. Both have hands outstretched and almost touch; it is an erotic pastiche of God and Adam on the ceiling of the Sistine Chapel.

And once more here is Pat, in clay, unfinished. Claire tests the small figurine with the tip of a finger. The clay crumbles to dust. Half of Pat's side is reduced to sand.

On an impulse Claire takes something from a low table, something especially beautiful. She believes it will be helpful.

One half of the studio is taken up with

rehearsal space, a practice barre in front of a large wall mirror, an upright piano, a tape deck, a few chairs, and mounted photographs of scenes from ballets.

Ken's half of the room complements Pat's. This is where he sketches and models her dancing, and this is where he undertakes his architectural and abstract work too. All is practical, clean, ordered, serious, and dedicated.

More than ever Claire feels that she should not be here. She is prying into Ken's soul. She is coming between Ken and Pat. However she climbs the staircase to the living area to pry further.

Here are the books. Huge handsome volumes of Breughel and Leonardo and Van Gogh. Thick and well-thumbed volumes on architecture and design. MacQuoid on English furniture, Dante illustrated by Doré, an astonishing Blake. And, less grandly, the pickings from second-hand stores, garage sales, Greyhound terminals. Here too are the casual snapshots of a love-affair. Ken and Pat at the beach, in a car in Vermont, on skis, clowning, kissing, loving. Who, Claire wonders, took them? Passing strangers?

She is jealous of the years Pat spent with Ken, of the knowledge Pat must have had of Ken's body when it was an extension of and not just an encumbrance to his mind. Guiltier than ever, she moves through to the bedroom.

White walls. Paintings bright with colour. A large double bed, and an open wardrobe. Within it Pat's clothes and Ken's clothes, side by side. Claire puts her arm into the midst of them, feels the coolness of silk, the roughness of tweed, the harshness of denim. She puts the sleeve of a sweatshirt to her face, and can smell, faintly but unmistakably, Ken.

But then there are light footsteps on the stairs, and Claire turns as Pat comes in. She wears a cloth coat over her leotard with a scarf around her neck, and still bears traces of her performance makeup. If she is surprised to see Claire in her bedroom she gives no hint of it.

'Oh, hi! Sorry I couldn't meet you. Dance and study and rehearse and take care of the studio and arrange business affairs. His work has become quite fashionable. I guess you already looked round?'

'Yes. Ken has a real gift.'

'Yes. He had.'

Pat sits at her dressing table, and, applying cold cream, removes what remains of her stage makeup. Seeing her face in the mirror, she makes deprecatory noises, but Claire can see no reason for them. To her Pat looks as good without makeup as with. She puts the key on the dressing table.

'I found the key where you said it would be.'

Pat looks at Claire in the mirror with some intensity. 'I'm going to close the old place up. Turn Ken's work over to a gallery. They will be better equipped to exploit it than I am.' Pat's movements are nervy and abrupt. She wipes her face clean of cosmetics as though punishing it.

'You'll have to excuse my rush. I'm late. I have a date.'

'I had to talk to you. You see, we're trying to find a way to help Ken Harrison.'

Pat watches Claire in the mirror as she says

brutally: 'The late Ken Harrison.'

'But he isn't ...'

'Yes, he is. He may not be to you. But he is to me. And to himself. Understand me, Doctor Scott, I loved the late Ken Harrison more than I have ever loved anyone, more than I intend to love anyone again, and I grieve for his death.'

'I can't believe you'll give him up so easily, Pat, so quickly.'

'Give him up? Ken Harrison is already gone. Look around you at the studio, at all this. *This* is Ken Harrison now.'

Pat is crying. But she continues to brush her hair and to apply her makeup – a hopeless task. Claire realises that Pat has retreated from her now, but persists:

'But he is unique, and that is why we've got to get him to change his mind.'

'You'll have to excuse me now,' says Pat. 'I'm late already.'

'I'm sorry.'

'It's very simple. I respect Ken's wishes because I respect him. Why don't you respect him too?'

'I do.'

'Then let him do what he wants to do. Quit tearing him to pieces. Let him go!'

Pat starts tearing up tissues. First she separates them into two thicknesses. Then she places them neatly in a pile, as a woman cutting sandwiches will. Then, hopelessly, she tears them relentlessly, any old how. The débris she scatters on the floor.

'If there's anything I can do,' Claire says, 'I don't mean about Ken necessarily. I mean about anything.'

'Oh, you can sort things out, can you? Can you turn time back? Can you make a truck stop at a red light? Or, if you can't do that, can you at least make it complete its work? Can you mend spines? That shouldn't be difficult for Wonderwoman. And how are you with cocks? Can you give a man back his self-respect? Can you at least make him feel like a man? And, if you can't do any of these things, what right do you have, doctor, to come snooping in here, taking away from me what little I have left, my privacy and my peace of mind. I'm sure you mean well, because that's your job, isn't it, to mean well? But after all, Ken's only one of hundreds of patients to you. You don't do so great with this one, well, you can easily find another one more amenable to your techniques. No shortage of patients, never will be, the one profession, medicine, with a built-in guarantee against redundancy, right?

'Yeah, well Ken was rather more than that to me. Maybe you've not been in love, Dr Scott. Looking at you, I dare say you are the sort of cold bitch who would not care to give herself freely as I did to Ken, give herself wholly, body and soul ... do you even know what I am talking about, I wonder? If Ken had asked me to do the worst thing in the world, torture a child, and had told me that it was necessary, I would have done it, and I think he would have done the same thing for me. We discussed this. People in love, Dr Scott, do discuss things, which less fortunate people never tangle with. We talked of who would die first and what would happen to the survivor. Seems kinda ironic now, huh?

'So I've told you something about how I loved

Ken, and love him, though Christ knows it's difficult enough, let me tell you about how I suffer for him. Do you know what people say about suffering, Dr Scott? Is that dealt with in the textbooks? They say it ennobles, right? Well, they're mistaken. Suffering doesn't ennoble, it degrades. I mean physically degrades too. I don't suppose you've ever seen me dance, have you? I was pretty good. Ken thought so. He knew about things like that, you see, anatomy and movement in space and – oh God what are you *doing* here?'

For a moment Pat looks at Claire, no longer at the tissues, and sees this strange cool woman, unacquainted with grief, and no longer feels hatred for her, just indifference, but there is still something left to be said, and she might as well say it as not.

'Yeah, I was good. Better than corps de ballet. And if I had stayed with Ken, if all this had not happened, I might have been the best. I was dancing, you see, for him. It was the best thing I had to give him, and I gave freely, the way you do when you're in love. It was an extension of our fucking. That's why I danced for him here, not just in the studio, and in the theatres. Only Ken saw how I could dance, only he knew. But how am I supposed to dance now, Dr Scott, with him lying there terrified and wretched and perpetually harassed by your lot? Let him die, for God's sake, let him die, not just for his own sake, but for mine. If he dies, I can dance for him again, we can be together again, but if this goes on – good Christ, have you any *idea* what it's like, what I've been talking about?'

Claire leaves her there then, surrounded by

fragments of tissue, and runs down the stairs, her fashionable shoes clattering on the carpetless stairs. She feels humiliated and ashamed. She has no idea what she will say to Emerson or to Ken. Later and in a calmer frame of mind, she analyses her emotions, as doctors tend to do, obsessively. She does not care for what she uncovers. Unmistakably her most passionate emotion is her naked jealousy of Pat.

*   *   *

Ken has begun to have doubts. At first he had had none. The pain had been too great, the prospect of never being free from it too over-powering. But he had imagined that it would have been quick and clean and easy, even pleasureable. Once he had read a story in which the hero had cut his wrists in a warm bath. As the blood had flowed out, spiralling into the water, a pleasant drowsiness had overtaken him, a lassitude, a sensation of utter contentment. Before he had had doubts Ken had not envisaged all this squabbling and in-fighting. Far too many dogs snarling over one paltry piece of meatless bone.

His doubts become more acute when he plays chess, for this is something at which he can compete on equal terms with anybody, a meeting of minds. His regular opponent, now that he is permitted – encouraged even – to spend more time in the Solarium, is a balding manic-depressive called Sackheim. Sackheim has the look of a man eating stale cheese. To Ken's surprise he does not play as one might expect a manic-depressive to play, with sudden brilliances interspersed with appalling oversights. His play is sound, steady and uninspired. On this particular morning, Ken realises why. Concealed from the view of his opponents Sackheim has a small chess computer, into which he has been feeding Ken's moves and from which he has received his own moves. Of course the problem for Sackheim, Ken realises, is that if the computer is to play at a reasonably fast speed he has to be programmed at a moderately low level of competence. Hence the powerful position in which Ken finds himself with a potentially overwhelming queen's side attack. Ken decides that the moment of truth has arrived.

'Foul! Foul play, Sackheim.'

'Can't stand losing, eh?' grunts Sackheim.

'It's not enough you move my pieces for me, you let that thing play for you too. Can't anyone do anything for himself round here?'

'Just checking the moves.'

'Cute, Sackheim, real cute. Queen to king's rook two, try feeding that one into Boris and see how he likes it.'

Sackheim punches the move into his computer, still keeping up the pretence of concealment. Boris considers all possibilities, doesn't care for any of them, and suggests: 'Resign!' Sackheim starts to replace the pieces in the box, while Emerson looms up behind him.

'Okay dammit,' says Sackheim, wondering whether there is any future in persecution mania, 'be that way. Tomorrow I'm playing with Frank Pierson.'

Ken can't believe his ears. 'But Frank's blind!'

'You know it!' Sackheim crows.

'Hello,' says Emerson. And to Ken: 'I thought we'd have a chat.'

'Have I a choice?'

Emerson wheels Ken out of the Solarium and onto the terrace.

'You must be the highest paid orderly in the business,' Ken says.

'Beats hell out of checking prostates.'

Ken remembers a joke told him by one of his students, an erstwhile medic who had jacked it all in. Emerson should be tough enough to take it.

'You know what a protoscope is, Doctor? It's a long tube with an arsehole at either end.'

'Very amusing, Ken,' says Emerson, who has heard it many times before, a little wearily.

They have reached the terrace railings. The weather could scarcely be pleasanter. The view of the city, with the bay in the background and yachts with brightly coloured sails in the bay, is seductive. Air and light and space. Well satisfied, Emerson says: 'Look at that view.' It sounds as though he owns it. Ken is automatically suspicious.

'It's not the first time I've seen it, Doctor, it doesn't make me want to live.'

'That being so,' Emerson says quietly. 'I have to tell you I'm committing you under the Mental Health Act.'

The sun is on Ken's face. The air is scented with autumn. Ken asks: 'Why is my life so important to you, Michael?'

'Because it is a life. It's sacred.'

'But *why?* What am I? My brain is running a mile a minute, but my body fails me. I haven't a

100

muscle with which to commit suicide! If I refuse to eat you'll feed me intravenously. Everything is pushed in and sucked out of me. And I have no say! I have no dignity. I have no person. In Northern Ireland they let the hunger strikers die, but I am not accorded the same privilege, although I am no criminal. Put yourself in my place. What would you do? That vaunted ego of yours would vanish and you'd feel the same as me.'

'You may be right,' says Emerson, then realises that he has been trapped into giving too much away, and hurries on. 'I mean about me. My ego. Maybe it is ego that makes me need to keep you alive. Maybe it's just because I happened to be in Emergency Reception when they wheeled you in. My bad luck or yours? Or maybe it's because I spoonfed you back to life with skill and knowledge and willpower. Is it my ego that makes me determined that you shan't throw away your life? Or is it the memory of the hundreds of patients I've seen who would endure anything for one more day on this earth, who would give anything to change places with you, if only that were possible?'

For a moment Ken looks out over the city where men and women lead lives of quiet desperation. He envies them. He says:

'I'd make that exchange gladly. Maybe it was your ego which saved my life, Doctor. Now respect my ego, and give it back to me.'

'I can't do that. I wish I could. I really wish I could. I can't. I can't.' He moves away from Ken, saying, without looking at him: 'I'll have an orderly take you back.'

In anger and frustration Ken begins to beat his head back against the pillow at first slowly, then with increasing violence, until a nurse runs up and gets an orderly to wheel him back into the hospital for immediate sedation.

* * *

While Ken is being fed his dinner by Mary Jo he thinks – and not for the first time – of one of the small but vital areas of personal freedom now lost to him for ever; the freedom to choose what to put on one's fork. There were certain combinations of food that once had given him pleasure. Mashed potato with melted butter and gravy over the top. Lettuce folded round a piece of liver. And other things. Now he has to eat in whatever sequence Mary Jo chooses. Chicken, peas, potatoes. She ignores the chicken skin. Ken feels it would be rather petty to protest. On the other hand he is extremely bored. (The food tastes of nothing anyway. Typical of hospitals. They commission reports from expensive nutrition experts. They work out diets based on carefully balanced calorific controls. And then they feed you food you can't eat.)

Suddenly he pipes up in a childish falsetto: 'How come there are no bunny rabbits on my bib?'

Mary Jo laughs, and shakes her head. A real nut case.

'I want bunny rabbits on my bib! Waa!'

'Come on, you crazy man, eat.'

She picks up the chicken drumstick and holds it

temptingly in front of his mouth. He snarls and takes a bite. She puts the drumstick back on the tray and licks her fingers. Ken laughs.

'Oh, that's great. I eat the drumstick and you lick your fingers.'

'Did I? Really?'

'You must be starving. Look, why don't *you* eat the drumstick and then lick *my* fingers?'

'Try the peas.'

'I hate peas. They're all clones. Once I used to be able to pick one out and say, "Now there's an unusual pea." You used to get pods with two or three really fat ones, or pods with just some squashed flat ones, and sometimes a whole row of tiny little ones scarcely bigger than their stems which you had to flick out with the back of your thumb nail. Remember? Nah, you're too young. Whatever happened to all those funny shaped peas? What would I give just to find a maggot in one?'

'Open up.'

'Is there no romance in your heart, Mary Jo?' But he does open up, and Mary Jo puts a forkful of peas into his mouth. Through the peas, Ken splutters: 'Hey, watch this. Make a circle with your thumb and forefinger.'

'Why?'

'Just do it, Mary Jo.'

Mystified and intrigued, she does as Ken has instructed her. He spits a pea at the circle, but it hits her hand.

'Hey, cut that out!'

'One more time. Please. I'm out of practice. If I don't practise how am I ever gonna make the Olympic training squad?'

Mary Jo makes another circle. Ken spits another pea.

'Bullseye! Bravo! Call Wide World of Sports, let's arrange a match. See if Helen Keller's available. Then a pro-celebrity tournament at Spitzbergen.'

'Come on, Ken, you've got to eat.' And she starts to feed him again.

'It's salty. Like tears.'

Mary Jo brings the glass of water with the bent straw to his lips. He takes a sip.

'Chateau Harris Reservoir, I think, with just a petulant hint of Lysol. A cheeky little vintage, wouldn't you say?'

* * *

For an insurance company lawyer who looks like a weasel, Carter Hill is proving to be surprisingly tough and resourceful. Ken would have been impressed had he seen him in Emerson's office. Ken would be impressed could he see him wining and dining Claire Scott in an intimate little restaurant which Not Everybody Knew About Yet.

Claire Scott does not need much persuasion to talk about Ken Harrison. Indeed she is much relieved to be able to do so. Outside the fevered atmosphere of the hospital, over some peaches flamed in brandy, she tells Carter about her visit to Ken's studio and about the extraordinary strength and wretchedness of the girl Pat. But as to what Ken has in mind to do:

'I hate it. I hate the whole idea. It's against all my training and instincts ...'

'But how would you feel if, by some miracle, Ken was given the use of his arms for thirty seconds, and swallowed a bottle of sleeping tablets?'

'I'd be ... relieved.'

'Would you try to save his life with a stomach pump?'

'I don't think so.'

'You might even arrange to have a bottle of pills handy and no one there?'

'There won't be any such miracle.'

'Maybe we ought to make suicide respectable again. As it is, there's always an inquest to find someone or something to blame. Why? Why can't a coroner simply say, "This man faced insuperable odds and he made a courageous decision. I record a verdict of noble death." '

'The Catholics have no such doubts. For them it's a mortal sin, and you know what that means. I may not agree with what Ken wants to do but I cannot think of him as a sinner.'

'To a lawyer there are no sinners; merely criminals.'

'And to a doctor merely the sick and the healthy.'

Later in Hill's car, an open-top MG which he drives like a family saloon, Hill says: 'Well, tonight has done one thing for me at least.'

'What?' Claire is slightly suspicious.

'It has made up my mind for me.'

'You're going to represent him?'

'Yes. Does that mean we're adversaries?'

'No, of course not.' And Claire puts a friendly

hand on Hill's arm. The lawyer looks sharply at her, and changes gear.

'I'm glad to hear it. In that case I've got a bottle of Remy Martin at my place just waiting for two non-adversaries. What say we –'

'Thanks, but –'

'Just a coupla blocks from here. A nightcap after a good dinner. Helen Reddy's greatest hits ...'

'Thanks, Carter, it's sweet of you, but no. Would you be really kind and drop me off at the hospital?'

Smiling ruefully, Carter Hill murmurs: 'That's what they always say.'

*   *   *

For the most part the hospital is dark. Isolated in circles of light, nurses read the latest Ed McBain thrillers and gasp with horror at what is going on in the 87th Precinct. Occasionally an intern is called into a hurried whispered consultation, a patient cries out in her sleep, a lavatory is flushed. But in the Intensive Care Unit, the lights are always on.

Claire Scott looks out of place in her belted grey dress, the dress in which she has just dined with Carter Hill, chosen for its simple elegance and which had so unexpected an effect upon the lawyer. She carries an oblong cardboard box along the hospital corridors, past the nurses' station, through the ICU, and into Ken's room, where Ken is asleep. He looks like a child. Claire places the box carefully on a small table and crosses to the bed. She arranges the sheets and blankets more comfortably around his body. Ken stirs. He has his back to her.

'Not two hours yet, nurse.'

'I thought I'd change your position anyway.'

'Oh, it's you. It should be the nurse.'

'Do you mind?' Claire moves round the bed, so that Ken can see her. He likes what he sees. Claire lets him look, then sits on the bed.

'I didn't expect to see you again tonight. You look real nice.'

'Thank you.'

'You didn't do all that just for me. Have you been out?'

'Yes, for dinner.'

'Good food? Good wine? Good company?'

'You're fishing.'

'You're so right.'

'Well, actually it was Carter Hill.'

'Hill? Well, well, the horny little bugger. Didn't take him long.'

'Just a dinner. Pasta. Fish. Peaches in brandy.'

'I know I asked him to represent me, but this is ridiculous. Peaches in *what?*'

'It was just a dinner.'

'Did my representative behave himself?'

'You were a perfect gentleman.'

'Maybe I had better hire another surrogate.'

'Ken ...'

Claire has dropped her flippant tone of voice. Ken notices the modulation with alarm. If she is going to get heavy with him, she should have let him sleep.

'Ken, uh ... I may have done something bad.'

'Something bad? This I want to hear.'

'Well, today, before meeting Carter Hill, I went to your studio.'

'My studio. What for?'

'Nothing sinister. I ... I wanted to know more about you.'

'What else is there to know. Nobody has ever examined me so thoroughly before. You've even seen the fluff inside my navel.'

'That's just the body, Ken ...'

'Don't knock it. From where I'm lying it seems pretty important. And I want you to know we've had some good times together, me and this body.'

'I'm glad I saw your studio work.'

Surprised, Ken says, 'Thank you.' He is touched by what seems to be the disinterested nature of the compliment. But then Claire adds:

'Wouldn't it be a good idea to have a piece or two of your sculpture here?' And he realises that, where Doctor Scott is concerned, it's all a part of the therapy.

'A good idea to be reminded of what I'll never do again? You really think so?'

'I'm sorry if I've upset you. But they're so good.'

'Help yourself to anything you want. Bound to be a good investment. Rarity value. When the news leaked out that Da Vinci was sinking fast, all the big Wall Street boys moved in.'

'Actually I did take one. Here it is.'

Claire proceeds to get the box and open it in front of him. Ken is reluctant to see it. What he was and what he could do is nothing to what he is now. But at the same time he cannot help but be curious to know which piece the woman will have chosen. From the box she takes reverently a white plaster hand.

108

'I hope you don't mind ...' says Claire.

Ken is astounded and impressed. He wants very much to reach out and touch it, though merely to see it again after so long is miraculous. But all he says is, 'You have excellent taste. It's certainly the best thing in the studio.'

'Oh, I'm glad.' Claire has received plenty of compliments in her time but can think of none which has given her so much pleasure.

'It's Michelangelo, of course. It's a realisation from the Sistine Chapel. The Finger of God bringing Adam and Eve to life.'

'What an idiot I am! I thought ... well, never mind, I'm sorry.'

'Don't be, please! I meant what I said about your taste. It's one of my favourites too. Actually I wouldn't mind looking at that.'

'I'm glad. I'll leave it.'

Claire places the hand where he can easily see it. It is all air and light and space. It glows from within. It gives him peace.

'I am delighted that you went to my studio, Claire.'

She sits on the bed again and smiles at him, a smile of great sweetness and much concern. She says, 'I'm beginning to think you're enjoying all this.'

'In a way I am. I tell you honestly, Claire, that for the first time in all these lousy months I feel just a little like a human being.'

'Isn't that the whole point? Isn't that what tonight has shown you? That you are a human being again. You're not fighting for death. I won't believe that.'

'Believe it! But you're right, Claire, I had to be

109

sure that I wanted to win this fight, and not just
to prove to myself that I'm alive.'

'And are you sure?'

'Oh yes, quite sure. Can you please do
something about this pillow? It's about as much
use as a bowl of custard.'

Claire takes the pillow from beneath his head,
plumps it up and replaces it. Their heads are very
close together. Ken talks to her as though to an
old friend. He has never seemed so vulnerable to
her before.

'Claire, for me life is over. I can't do the things I
want to do, so I won't say the things I want to
say. So it had better end. You understand?'

Claire nods. She understands; too well.

'So on with the fight!' Ken cries, quite
cheerfully.

'Goodnight, Ken, sweet dreams.'

'Goodnight, Claire. Claire ...'

'Yes?'

'Are you driving home?'

'Yes.'

'Use your seat belt.'

*   *   *

It is not easy keeping track of time. Ken's life is
punctuated by dialysis and by enemas, by tests
and by therapy, by plastic food. There is nothing
significant to distinguish night from day, morning from evening. He listens to music on
headphones, and knows the length of a sym-
phony better than the length of a day. When he is
too troubled and frightened to be calmed by

110

music, he rests his eyes on the hand of God. He comes to worship it.

Consequently the night of John's disco may have been the night following Claire's off-duty visit, or the night following the night following, or the night following *that*, but it is certainly a night to remember.

John arrives at Ken's bedside unexpectedly, for he is not supposed to be on duty, and straps Ken into his special wheelchair with strict instructions: 'You keep that flapper shut closed, man, you hear me good.'

'Why? Where are ...'

'Shut *closed*.'

Whistling 'Marching Through Georgia', and with an expression on his seraphic face of butter *not* melting in his mouth, John pushes Ken past the nurses' station, and towards the elevators. The duty nurse looks up in surprise from his copy of *Penthouse*, but when John says, 'Dialysis', without breaking his stride, the duty nurse seems satisfied. Ken begins to enjoy himself. While waiting for the elevator to arrive, John repeats in a hoarse whisper: 'Shut closed,' and then they are safely in the elevator. When they reach the basement Mary Jo, in brown slacks, and a white polo-neck, her brown curls hanging loose, so that Ken scarcely recognises her from her uniformed self, is waiting for them. Then begins a wild dash through the corridors of hell. Mary Jo runs ahead, pushing the swing doors open for the chair to crash through. There is strange machinery, huge tubes, wires and wheels on all sides. Dim lights do no more than cast weird shadows. Ken's head turns from side to side in amazement and wonder as he rides this hospital ghost-train until at last the final doors crash shut behind them, they round a corner and emerge into –

'Paradise!'

Ken's hyperbole is understandable. What seems to him to be paradise is, in fact, a basement storage room, converted for the occasion into a disco. Four musicians, unkempt and perilous-looking, are warming up their instruments. A xylophone awaits John who whips off his white overalls to reveal a bizarre outfit of frilled shirt, black waistcoat and jewellery. As soon as John gets his sticks in his hands, the group goes into action.

'Fantastic!' cries Ken as Mary Jo wheels him into the centre of the cluttered space, and John, still playing, introduces him to the group.

'The attachment to the wheelchair is Ken Harrison, otherwise known as the Talking Head. Ken, meet the Steelies. Papa Joe on lead guitar, Big Willie on bass – hey, how did ya get that name? Gay Frank, a good friend in a tight spot, on keyboards, and Placido on the steel drums. Let it go!'

And so they do. The music dazzles Ken's ears. While they play, John, Big Willie and Placido light joints and soon the air is humming with the sweet smell of the scented weed. At the end of the number, Mary Jo applauds and makes a request.

'Play the one you did last night, John.'

'Which one?'

And Mary Jo hums a snatch of it, moving prettily to the beat. *Last night*, Ken thinks, what have I been missing?

'Got it,' cries Papa Joe, and picks out a melody

to which the others add rhythm and harmony. John sticks a joint between Ken's lips, and Ken takes in a deep pull, but Mary Jo, looking as stern as Rodriguez, is quick and snatches the cigarette away.

'Oh, *c'mon*,' says Ken aggrieved. 'A toke for the kid here, huh?' But Mary Jo is quite determined.

Then the band goes into 'Punkette Nights' and the sound and the smoke imbue Ken with a feeling of carefree well-being. It is all so easy. They should do it in the wards. He focusses his eyes on the glitter of the instruments, on the way a guitar string vibrates, on the patterns of smoke in air.

'Great, really great, you know,' he mutters vaguely to anyone who might be listening, but the musicians are playing, and Mary Jo has slipped out of the room. 'Great.'

Ken has been more of a party-giver than a party-goer, perhaps because the studio was a perfect venue for a party. He would invite the most interesting and glamorous students and cater the food. A huge bowl of chicken and rice, another of fruit. Chilled wine with the frost still on the bottle and, in the early hours, hot pizza. He would select the music with care. Little Richard or Jerry Lee Lewis to get things hopping, then something cooler and quieter, Miles Davis or Monk, to allow things to happen, and then always at the end a tune of Bechet's so mellifluous, so haunting that it would stay in the students' heads and dazzle their minds.

'That music,' they would say, 'at Ken's party, what *was* it?' And friendships formed while that music played – he would never tell them what it was, lest they played it too often and at insignificant or inappropriate moments – would last.

But it wouldn't have done now, Ken could not have borne it; under the circumstances a punk xylophone was just the job.

Halfway through the third number Mary Jo bursts back into the room.

'Someone's coming!'

'Who was it said the building was sound-proofed?' asks John plaintively. But the musicians are unfazed, and seem to be quite prepared for an interruption, at least to judge by the speed and efficiency with which they grab their instruments and make their getaways. Ken watches them do so with a partially drug-induced feeling of irresponsibility and unconcern. John has trouble with his xylophone, no easy thing to pack away. Mary Jo does her best to help him, but is inclined to giggle, and, as the voice of a security guard comes gradually closer, it seems odds on exposure and disgrace. However, just as the guard opens one of the doors to the storage room, John, Mary Jo and the xylophone clatter and ping their way out through the other door. All the guard sees is Ken alone in his wheelchair in a room full of suspiciously scented smoke. He exhibits curiosity and anger in roughly equal proportions. Ken, floating, as it seems to him, several feet above his chair, greets the guard with courtesy.

'Good evening to you, sir.'

The guard is altogether less courteous. 'Who are you? What are you doing here?' His speech is slightly slurred. Ken offers an explanation of sweet reasonableness. 'Inspecting the plumbing. Consider it condemned.' He cannot understand why the guard gets so angry.

*   *   *

Ken never supposed the time would come when he would regard a hangover as a privilege, but then he never supposed a lot of things about himself which have come to pass. Six months paralysed in bed chastens a man. But the morning after the jam session in the basement he does feel hungover and he does feel privileged.

Mary Jo is also not looking her best. Rodriguez is ominously quiet and not as gentle as usual when it comes to taking Ken's blood pressure and other such domestic matters.

Mary Jo is making the bed. First she rolls Ken onto his side, so that one half of the bed is clear. Then she pulls up the sheets on that side, and tucks in the fresh ones. As she rolls Ken over onto the clean sheets, preparatory to completing the bed making, he groans and says:

'Five, four, three, two, one, zero. We do not have lift-off, thank the Lord. Rodriguez, my beloved guardian angel, do you suppose you could let me have about thirty or forty aspirin, please? On the other hand, fifty would do.'

'How about one?'

'Two? My lawyer is coming this morning, and if you want to keep my blood pressure within reason ...'

'Nobody cares about my blood pressure,' Rodriguez complains. She busies herself flexing

Ken's arms, wrists and hands, while Mary Jo finishes making the bed.

'The question you've all been waiting for,' says Rodriguez.

'Big money prize?'

'What were you all doing in the basement?'

'Sunning myself?' suggests Ken. Mary Jo looks away hurriedly, not being able to trust herself to keep a straight face.

'Your breath, Mr Harrison, smells like my whole neighbourhood on a hot Sunday when the garbage men are on go-slow.'

At this Carter Hill enters, unannounced. From where he lies, held by Mary Jo, Ken can only see the lawyer from the waist down.

'Who's that? Can't be a doctor. Doctors wear Italian loafers and silk socks.'

'It's Carter Hill,' says Carter Hill apologetically.

'Ah yes, the guy who sues, eats and chases women for me. The professional surrogate. And who also needs a shoe-shine.'

'How are you feeling this morning, Ken?'

'Great. Wonderful,' says Ken, then groans as Mary Jo rolls him back onto the sheets.

'Turn them slower,' says Rodriguez. 'They get dizzy easily. Lack of circulation.'

'Yeah, don't circulate much anymore,' says Ken. 'Only move in ever decreasing circles these days. One day I could disappear up my own catheter. Nasty. Well, Carter Hill, what's your decision?'

'Actually I –'

But before he can give his decision, John comes in with the breakfast tray. For Ken's benefit he hums:

Thursday may be awful sweet
But Friday's dancin' time for me
On my feet (feet, feet, feet)
On my feet (feet, feet, feet)

'Ole brown eyes,' mutters Ken disparagingly.

'Nice,' says Hill, admiring the Hand of God.

Says John: 'How are we feeling this morning, Mr Harrison?'

To Carter Hill's mystification the black orderly and the young nurse start to giggle uncontrollably. Rodriguez however looks like a thundercloud about to shed its load, for she has guessed who took Ken to the basement. Maintaining a straight face, Ken asks Carter Hill again for his decision.

'Yes,' says Hill.

Ken exhales, takes a deep breath. 'Okay, when do we get our hearing?'

'I haven't applied for it yet.'

'Oh, and why have you not?'

'Two reasons. First, commitment judges will usually find for the hospital. Second, I think I have something better.'

'Now *that* sounds interesting. What is it?'

Mary Jo has been taking her time over the bed. She is desperate to hear what passes between Ken and Carter Hill, and Rodriguez knows it.

'Sadler, get an aspirin please,' says Rodriguez with a smile of great sweetness. Mary Jo sighs and smiles sympathetically at Ken, who mouths the word 'two' at her. Mary Jo nods and trots off with a backward glance as she closes the door. Rodriguez is rolling the covers over Ken, a simple task which would not normally detain her long, but she too is curious.

'Did Dr Emerson order you to stay with me while my lawyer is here?' Ken asks, suddenly suspicious.

'I just should be available in case you get too excited.' Rodriguez is not used to being on the defensive, and finds it an uncomfortable experience.

'Rodriguez, you're the one who gets me excited.' Increasingly flustered, the Puerto Rican reaches under the bed covers. 'Not now Rodriguez. Wait until we're alone.' This has the effect of embarrassing Carter Hill as well as Rodriguez, who is, after all, only taking Ken's pulse. 'For a moment there,' says Ken, 'I thought I was going to get lucky. Maybe, if you were to take her out to dinner, Carter, you might soften her up a little. She has a weakness for peaches flamed in brandy. Fifteen ... sixteen ... seventeen ... eighteen ...' And Rodriguez gives up trying to take his pulse. Thereupon Ken becomes immediately businesslike, and asks Carter Hill:

'What's "better"? What do you have in mind?'

'Well, Mr Harrison, I want to go for a writ of habeas corpus.'

'Habeas corpus? I thought that had to do with criminals.'

'Usually it does,' says Hill, and then breaks off. Mary Jo has reappeared, smiling cheerfully and with two aspirins in a paper cup. Rodriguez takes one of the aspirins and pops it into Ken's mouth, then glares, hands on hips, at Mary Jo, until the unfortunate girl is glared out of the room. Ken sips water while Carter Hill continues. 'It's against the law to deprive anyone of his liberty without due process. If that happens, he can apply for a writ of habeas corpus, which means "give us the body".'

'In my case,' says Ken, 'it couldn't be more appropriate.'

'And if sufficient cause can't be established to detain the individual, the judge will order his release.'

'How long will it take?'

'Not long. It's one of the few legal processes that moves very quickly. A couple of days. I'll have time for a shoe-shine, but not much more.'

'Will I have to go to court?'

'I doubt it. I should think that any judge will agree to set the place of hearing in the hospital.'

'So,' says Ken, very much afraid, and particularly afraid of being afraid, 'all's well that ends.'

Rodriguez, unable to find any more odd jobs with which to occupy herself, leaves the room. Hill picks up his briefcase and tucks it under his arm.

'I'm off to find a judge. See you soon.'

But before he can go, Ken breaks in with: 'It will be an unusual case for you – making a plea for your client's death.'

'I'll be honest with you, Mr Harrison. It's a case I could bear to lose.'

'If you do lose, it's a life sentence for me.'

Hill tries to find something else to say, but the courtesies of polite conversation seem inappropriate. He is about to put a comforting hand on Ken's arm, when the thought that Ken will be unable to feel it makes him self-conscious about the gesture. He goes.

*

119

Is it that night, or early the following morning? Is it another night altogether? The room is dark, except for a sliver of light through drawn curtains. The light seems drawn to the Hand of God, which glows like a child's face. A student nurse comes in, moving with extreme caution. One can tell that she hasn't been at the job for long. She leaves the light off, but the door ajar, as she moves to Ken's side to turn him. Ken has been dreaming that he was skiing down the side of a mountain. Regularly now he has dreams of motion, skiing, sailing, wind-surfing, bicycling, jogging, although he had never been keen on most of these activities. The worst times of all are when he has such dreams and wakes. Or when he has dreams of sexual promise, always frustrated by his incapacity.

The new nurse is a Puerto Rican like Rodriguez, but younger, twenty maybe. It seems to Ken that she has a kind face.

'You can turn on the light if you want to,' says Ken. Pat had said that to him once a long time ago. But the girl leaves the room in semi-darkness as she turns him firmly but gently. Ken feels nothing.

'You're new. What's your name?'

'Stella.'

'You're very kind. A lot of nurses come in and yank you around until you're thoroughly awake. Then they disappear for another two hours, or until such time as you've managed to get off to sleep again.'

A little shyly, Stella asks: 'You're trying to be released, aren't you? To be taken off medication?'

'Everybody knows about it then?'

'Oh yes.'

Ken stares into the gloom trying to make out the girl's dusky face, shielded by darkness. He can see the whites of her eyes. She says: 'Aren't you afraid?'

Scarcely audible, Ken says: 'Yes.'

She moves away from the bed, out of the room. He sees her silhouette momentarily before she shuts the door. Ken stays awake.

PART 4
HABEAS CORPUS

Mary Jo has groomed him, and John has trimmed his moustache and beard. Somebody in the hospital administration has gone to the trouble of acquiring a new bathrobe – a natty number in a brown tartan check – for him. When one considers how many requisition forms and signatures, how many memos and reminders this must have involved, it becomes apparent that the case of the hospital versus Harrison is acquiring the status of a Watergate.

The effect of it all is to make Ken nervous. In the circumstances it is not strange that he should be nervous, but these nerves are akin to stage-fright, the result of Ken finding himself centre-stage and in the spot-light with no very clear idea of his lines or his cues.

'Don't I at least get to order a special last breakfast?' he asks John.

'Hey, man,' says John, 'you hear about the woman who beat up her husband? In court she tells the judge: "When he finally got me all hot and bothered, I pulled up my frock, and, Judge, he wasn't ready! No more ready than you are this minute, Judge!"' Ken laughs. 'You ready?'

'Guess so.'

John makes as if to look at his watch. 'Five, four, three, two, one, here we go!' And he pushes Ken into the corridor.

As they pass the nurses' station, Rodriguez and

125

Mary Jo stare at him with grave concern. Ken
gives them a wink.

'Aren't you ladies gonna wish me luck?'

'No,' says Rodriguez.

'I wish you luck,' says Mary Jo, but rather
sadly.

'Thanks, Joey. Hey, John, where are we off to?'

'Not dialysis. This time to the library. They got
the place all fixed up real nice. Even got the judge
a big comfortable chair on account of they figured
that if he had to sit listening to some miserable
jive-ass moaning on about wanting to die, the
least they could do was make him comfortable.
Hey, you hear about the case of the mad axeman?
"Judge, he just reached over and hit him in the
ass." "You mean rectum?" "Well, it didn't do him
no real good!"'

Carter Hill is having a less entertaining
journey to the hospital library. The nurses
recognise him, and look away. He is a pariah.
Emerson passes him and gives him a curt nod.
Hill puts a hand on Emerson's arm.

'Doctor, I want you to know that no matter
what the decision of the court, I'm truly sorry
we've been forced into such a distasteful
situation.'

'It's not over yet, Hill. I'm certain the law isn't
so stupid as to let my patient die.'

'And I'm just as certain that the law isn't so
stupid as to allow anyone, even an eminent
doctor, arbitrary power over other human beings.'

'My power is not arbitrary. It has been earned
with knowledge and skill. The law is not qualified
to judge a purely professional issue.'

'That's what it's always doing.'

126

'Suppose you win,' says Emerson, looking Hill in the eye, a look which a generation of young doctors have flinched away from, 'and suppose that with his dying breath Ken Harrison changes his mind. Consider that.'

'That's what the law is there to do. Consider all possibilities.'

*   *   *

Hill and Ken meet at the door to the hospital library.

'Nervous?' asks Hill.

'Me? No. You?'

'You bet.'

A bleak-looking man approaches them along the corridor.

'Oh this, Ken, is Mr Eden, attorney for the hospital.'

Eden starts to shake hands, then quickly stops himself.

'How do you do, Mr Harrison?'

'You have terrific reflexes.'

'Yes ... I ... er ...'

And the strangely assorted threesome enters the library.

There are books in the library, a few, much thumbed, for the use of the patients; others, pompously bound medical tomes, for the use of the staff and less thumbed. There is a table and a fine large chair for the judge. There is a table and chair for the stenographer. There is a table and chairs for the opposing lawyers. There is a chair for the witnesses. If one may make a correlation between the quality of justice administered and the amount of furniture necessary for its administration, there is little doubt that this will be an example of the highest traditions of American law. Ken, of course, comes with his own chair, which, at a nod from Carter Hill, John wheels over to the biggest of the tables. The doctors, Emerson, Scott and Barrows, who have been in consultation together, acknowledge his arrival. Emerson and Barrows smile; Scott tries to. John leaves.

There is a loud knock which ought to signify the entrance of the Judge, but it is only the Court Clerk. But when that dignitary announces the arrival of Judge Wyler, all rise to honour him, and it is hard not to be impressed. He makes an imposing figure, stout but not flabby, with steely-grey hair, and the look of a man accustomed to being obeyed. His manner, however, is unexpectedly brisk and conversational.

'Please sit down. This is an informal hearing, which I should like to keep as brief as possible.' When the Judge sits, all sit. 'Mr Kenneth Harrison.'

'Yes, sir.' Ken's voice is not quite steady.

'I've decided in consultation with Mr Eden and Mr Hill not to subject you to examination and cross-examination.'

'Sir, I would like to be able to say ...'

'Don't work yourself up, Mr Harrison, we have a long way to go. If I have any doubts – and I usually do have – I shall question you myself. Doctors Scott, Emerson and Barrows?'

Emerson is not slow in getting to his feet. 'This is Scott, Your Honour, and Dr Barrows. It follows

that I am Emerson.' There are nods and cautious
smiles all round.

'Now, doctors, if there should be any medical
reason to interrupt the proceedings, do so
whenever it is necessary. Dr Emerson, will you
take the oath, please?'

While the Clerk reads the words of the oath and
Emerson does so solemnly swear, the stenographer rests her fingers. From her point of view
she wishes there were more and longer oaths to be
sworn at regular intervals throughout court
cases. Still, holding the case in a hospital makes
a change, and what she has seen of the
depositions suggests that this is to be an unusual
hearing in other ways too. Heigh-ho. Back to
work.

At the Clerk's instruction, Emerson sits in the
witness chair while Eden rises to his feet.

'Dr Emerson, what is your position here?'

'I'm Chief of Medical Service.'

'Would you care to give the court a medical
history of Mr Harrison's treatment here?'

'Yes indeed. Following an automobile accident
on the evening of May the twenty-seventh, Mr
Harrison was admitted in shock and suffering
from a fractured left tibia, fractured right tibia
and fibula, fractured pelvis, four fractured ribs,
one of which had punctured the right lung, and a
dislocated fourth cervical vertebra which had
crushed the spinal cord. He also suffered internal
damage to spleen and kidneys, for which we
performed a splenectomy and double nephrec-
tomies. He remained unconscious for thirty hours.
As a result of treatment here, all the bones and
ruptured tissue have healed with the exception of

the spinal cord and this, together with mental trauma, is all that remains of the initial trauma.'

'Dr Emerson, will there be improvement in the spinal cord?'

'I regret not.'

'Kidney function?'

'No.'

'And the mental trauma?'

'It is impossible to violate the body to the extent to which Mr Harrison's has been violated and not suffer severe mental aberration, depression, even loss of reality and hallucination.'

Wyler's technique when he wishes to interrupt is to clear his throat in a long, low rumbling fashion. This gives lawyers time to conclude sentences, but witnesses do not always take the hint. Emerson does not, and Wyler has to raise his hand, an impressive procedure.

'In your view, is Mr Harrison suffering from such mental aberration?'

'He's certainly depressed.'

'Clinically depressed?'

'Clinically depressed, yes.'

Eden thanks Dr Emerson and sits down. He does not feel inclined to thank Judge Wyler, however, for the Judge represents a very unhealthy judicial trend. In his opinion there are too many judges around who like to fancy that they are still attorneys at law and undertake the questioning of witnesses themselves. How is a young man to get himself noticed under such conditions? It never happened to James Stewart, Spencer Tracy or Orson Welles in their films. Why does it have to happen to him?

Wyler calls on Carter Hill, who makes great

play out of opening his briefcase, extracting documents therefrom, closing his briefcase, and looking around the library (with a particular smile for Dr Scott), before starting his questions.

'Doctor Emerson, is there any way in which you can demonstrate this clinical depression? Any tests or measurements you can show us?'

'No.'

'Then how do you distinguish clinical depression, which might preclude the ability to make informed and logical decisions, from a perfectly sane, justified feeling of depression as a result of existing conditions?'

'That's easy,' Emerson retorts with a hint of smugness. 'By relying on my eighteen years as a physician dealing with both types.'

Hill wipes his nose with a perfectly folded handkerchief which he then replaces in his top pocket. To those who know Hill this presages a leading question.

'Are you a psychiatrist, Dr Emerson?'

'No.'

'Have you any degrees or credentials in that area of medical practice? Have you had any specialised training in psychiatry?'

'No.'

'No further questions, Dr Emerson.'

Wyler: 'Mr Eden?' But Eden shakes his head. 'We are most grateful to you, Dr Emerson, but you are now excused.'

From his demeanour one might suppose that Dr Emerson does not wish to be excused, is not used to being excused, and deeply resents being excused, but he really has no option but to step down.

While Dr Barrows is being called and sworn in, a small and insignificant door in the library is eased open, and John, shedding one dimension from his customary three, sidles into the room. He is not observed. He sits down quietly between Glauber's Salts and Glaucoma.

Carter Hill continues the proceedings. 'Dr Barrows, what position do you hold, and where?'

'I'm a consulting psychiatrist at Monroe State Mental Hospital.'

'Then in the course of your professional life you must see a large number of patients suffering from depressive illness.'

'Yes, I do.'

'You've examined Mr Harrison?'

Judge Wyler clears his throat, and Hill looks nervously down at his notes while the Judge comments waspishly: 'Well, we know that, or else why would he be here? Remember the word "informal", Mr Hill.'

'Yes, Your Honour. Now, Dr Barrows, would *you* say that Mr Harrison is suffering from a depressive illness?'

'No, I would not.'

'The court has heard evidence that Mr Harrison is depressed. Do you dispute that?'

'No, but depression is not necessarily an illness. In my opinion Mr Harrison's depression is reactive rather than endogenous.'

'Endogenous meaning originating within the body?'

'That's correct. In other words he's reacting in a perfectly rational manner to a very bad situation.'

'No further questions,' says Hill, well satisfied.

But Ken has seen too many courtroom movies to feel optimistic yet. Besides which Eden has yet to show his hand. Now he rises.

'Doctor, is there any objective evidence that you can produce to prove that Mr Harrison is entirely capable?'

'There are clinical symptoms of endogenous depression. Disturbed sleep patterns, loss of appetite, lassitude, and many more, but, even if they were present, they would be masked by Mr Harrison's physical condition.'

'Then how can you be sure that this is, in fact, a reactive depression?'

'By experience naturally. And by discovering when I talked with him that he has a remarkably incisive mind and is perfectly capable of understanding his position and deciding what he wants to do about it.'

Quietly and conversationally Eden asks: 'Doctor Barrows, do you think Mr Harrison has made the right decision?'

Quickly Carter Hill is on his feet. 'Your Honour, is that relevant?'

Wyler considers for a moment. Then: 'No. Not really.'

But Barrows says: 'I'd like to answer that if I may.'

'All right, go ahead,' says the Judge.

Barrows is dark-skinned and balding. He is enormously dignified, more so even than Judge Wyler. 'No,' he says. 'I think Mr Harrison has made the wrong decision.'

Astonished and angry at this betrayal, Ken cries out: 'Bullshit!'

The Judge almost smiles: 'Mr Harrison, when I

said informal, I didn't mean uncontrolled. Now be quiet.'

Eden is happy to conclude his cross-examination. Wyler invites Hill to come back at Barrows. Hill asks:

'But though you may disagree with Mr Harrison's decision, you still confirm that he has no diminished capacity, nor does he lack sufficient facts to make a sane, intelligent and informed decision?'

'I do so confirm.'

'Thank you, Dr Barrows,' says Wyler. 'I think that will be all.'

As Barrows leaves the library, the Judge takes a document from his case and studies it.

'I have here the sworn deposition of Dr Jacobs, the consultant psychiatrist for the hospital, who was unable to be with us today. It agrees with Dr Emerson's position.' He hands the deposition to the Clerk. 'Have it entered in the record.'

'Yes, Your Honour.'

'And now, Mr Harrison, do you feel like answering some questions from me?'

Ken looks sharply at the Judge, whose expression is impenetrable. Curious to think that so much depends upon this man. Who *is* he? Who chose him for the job? How did their lives come to be so entangled?

'Yes, Your Honour, I do.'

'Do you think you will be able to control yourself?'

Ken smiles. 'That depends on the questions.'

'Well, Mr Harrison,' says the Judge with quaint formality, 'I shall do what I can to avoid making them inflammatory.'

'You're far too kind.'

'Not at all.'

'No, I mean it. I should have preferred a hanging judge.'

'Well, Mr Harrison, it occurs to me that whatever I may decide I am just that.'

'Swear in the witness.'

'Raise your right hand,' says the Clerk, then realises his *faux pas*. He has to come round the table and lift Ken's hand for him, placing the Bible under it. Much embarrassed, he then lifts the wrong hand. The Judge recalls an occasion when a witness in his court was sworn in on a nicely bound copy of a book entitled *Home Mechanics for the Handyman*. These things happen and, in his experience, the authority of the law is not diminished by being seen to have a human face. He worries about the present case however, which seems to promise no satisfactory outcome.

'Now, Mr Harrison, the Medical Director and a consulting psychiatrist claim that you're not capable of making an informed, intelligent decision.'

'They're wrong.'

'Maybe. Do *you* think you're suffering from depression?'

'I would be insane if I were not depressed.'

'But wanting to die must be strong evidence that your mental state has gone far beyond simple depression.'

'I don't want to die.'

Astonished, Judge Wyler raises both arms in an uncharacteristically histrionic gesture, and asks: 'Then what the hell is this case all about?'

Eden smirks and Carter Hill glances up in surprise. The Judge turns to the stenographer. 'Make that read, "Then what is this case all about?" if you will be so kind.'

Ken says: 'I had a "hell" and a "bullshit" before. Maybe she could cross those out too.' Judge Wyler clears his throat ominously, so that Ken thinks it best to apologise, which he does with a small smile. After a moment collecting his thoughts together, Ken continues:

'I don't want to die because, as far as I'm concerned, Your Honour, I am already dead. I just want the doctors to recognise that my condition doesn't constitute a life in any sense of the word.'

'Legally, you're alive,' Wyler interposes.

'I could even challenge that. Any reasonable definition of life must include the idea of its being self-supporting. In heart transplant cases it's legal to take someone's heart if they need respirators and all that other medical hardware to keep them alive.'

'There also has to be absence of any brain activity. Your brain is certainly working.'

'Working and sane.'

'That, Mr Harrison, is what we are here to decide.'

'I'm not asking anyone to kill me. I realise that that would put the doctors in an impossible position. I just want to be discharged from the hospital.'

'Which will kill you.'

'Then that proves my point. I'll spend the rest of my life in the hospital with everything geared to keep my brain alive, and there never will be the slightest possibility for it to direct anything at all. This is an act of deliberate cruelty, indefinitely extended.'

'Wouldn't it be more cruel for society to let people die when, with some effort, it could save them?'

'No. Not more cruel. Just as cruel.'

'Then why should the hospital let you die, if it's just as cruel?'

'The cruelty is not a question of saving someone or letting them die. The cruelty is in not allowing the person concerned to make the choice. I should like to be able to decide what happens to my own body. I demand the right to decide its fate!'

'But a man who is desperately depressed is not capable of making a reasonable choice.'

'That, as you said, Your Honour, is the question to be decided.'

'Very well then, you tell me why your decision to die is a reasonable choice.'

Claire Scott thinks of the visit she paid to Ken's studio, of the books and the pictures, the sculptures, the clothes and Pat. An active life, a useful life, a loving life; a life that contained, it seemed, all that anybody could ask of life, and more than all but a handful could expect. And then she remembers the night in Ken's room when she had realised the extent of his pain and her inability to help. 'I can't do the things I want to do,' he had said, 'so I won't say the things I want to say.' Since then he has retreated from her, from all of them, as he had retreated from Pat, because there are some burdens one can only bear for oneself. Now for the first time she wants him to win, she wants it to be finished quickly. Now for the first time, although there is no more she can do for him she is on his side. Ken is talking as though to himself:

'The best part of my life was, I suppose, my work. The most valuable asset that I had was my imagination. The tragedy is that my mind was not paralysed along with my body. Because you see my imagination – which is my most precious possession – has become my enemy. It tortures me constantly, when I am awake and when I am asleep, with thoughts of what might have been and of what might be to come. And because of this I can feel my mind slowly decaying too. Women, for example. I loved them. I loved what they were, the look of them, the way they thought, the way they smelt, everything they represented. Now I dread it when they come into the room because I loathe the way they make me feel. You know, what fills me with outrage and despair is that you, Judge Wyler, who have no connection with me whatever, have the right to condemn me to a life of torment because you can't *see* the pain. There's no blood and there's no screaming. But if you saw a mutilated animal on the side of the road, you'd shoot it, wouldn't you? Well, I'm asking for no more than that you show me the same mercy you'd show an animal. But I'm not asking you to commit an act of violence; it's really very easy for you. All you have to do is take me somewhere and just leave me. But if in your wisdom and with the full authority of the law behind you, you don't, then I hope you will come back here in five years time and see what a piece of work you did today.'

Although he has finished speaking Ken neither

138

takes his eyes off the Judge nor moves a muscle. The stenographer brings her transcript up to date, and the room becomes quite silent. Carter Hill appears to be studying some official document, and John, unobserved, is recalling the wild night in the basement, when all the despair seemed to have been wiped off Ken's face, as a child's face is wiped clean with a sponge. Claire Scott is in tears.

The Judge rises.

'In hearings for a writ of habeas corpus, an immediate decision is mandated, but I propose to consider the issues carefully for a while. Therefore I request everyone to remain close at hand until my return, unless a medical emergency pre-empts your presence.'

* * *

In the nurses' station Mary Jo is putting instruments into the steriliser. Suddenly, she stops, and freezes, and anxiety clouds her eyes. She looks at her watch. They should have finished by now. She feels the need to say a prayer, but is not sure what she should pray for. Eventually she asks that whatever the outcome it should be what is best for Ken, whether he knows what is best for himself or not. She remembers him spitting peas, and smiles.

* * *

Judge Wyler has been telephoning his office from

139

the public call box in the hospital (such graffiti!)
and asking them to pass on to him information
about certain precedents which may help him in
arriving at a decision. Now that he has all the
information he needs, he has reached his
decision, but lingers awhile on the hospital
terrace. The first snow of winter is threatening,
and he watches the gusts of his breath, and,
below in the gardens, patients and relatives
walking and talking. The air is marvellously
fresh after the mustiness of the library. He is
reluctant to return indoors.

*   *   *

Rodriguez has been filling out forms in the
nurses' station. Why is so much of her time taken
up with forms? She had never supposed, when
she started her training, that she would turn into
a form-filler. 'Stupid,' she mutters. Her mind is
not on her forms however. It must be time now.
Soon the news of the Judge's decision will be all
over the hospital. She knows what they ought to
decide, but there is no guarantee they will.
Lawyers! Spend too much time filling out forms,
that's their trouble. She sees Mary Jo frozen in
immobility.
 'What do you think you are paid for, child? To
sleep on your feet? To work, to work!' And she
claps her hands several times in quick succession.

*   *   *

Ken remains in the library and shakes his head violently when John offers to push him out into the corridor for a smoke. He is concentrating on the past. He is trying to recall in exact detail the look and feel of that huge construction he had been working on at the time of the accident. It had been finished, hadn't it? Not perfect, but then nothing ever was. A fair attempt which had gone some way towards proving what he had set out to prove. And the children, with only a little prompting, had played on and in and around it. That was when he knew it had succeeded. Did they still use it in their games? Did they prefer it to the pile of old motor tyres and the water barrel? Perhaps John or Mary Jo could find out and let him know. He can remember the hiss and flare of the oxyacetylene lamp, the smell of the mask, the roughness of the metal. He can remember being satisfied, and therefore happy. It is something to have such a memory; something he must hold onto for as long as he can. Soon they will be returning, and the Judge will deliver his verdict. A life sentence in either case. But until then he must hold on to that, he must hold on ...

*　　*　　*

'There are precedents aplenty for both sides of this issue,' says Judge Wyler, when the court has reassembled, and all, including Emerson, are seated. 'In re Quinlan, the Supreme Court of New Jersey recognised the presentation of the personal right to privacy against bodily intrusions. In Belchertown versus Salkewicz, the court held

141

that the right to refuse medical treatment in appropriate circumstances extends to both competent and incompetent persons. This case also established in Massachusetts the authority of the Courts in all matters where there is a dispute over the right of an individual to refuse medical treatment. And the law holds that a deliberate decision to embark on an action which will eventually lead to death is not ipso facto evidence of insanity. If it were, society would have to condemn many men to dishonourable burial rather than posthumous medals. Yet we do have to remember that Mr Harrison's mind is affected and we must, in this case, be most careful not to allow Mr Harrison's intelligence to blind us to the fact that he may be suffering from a depressive illness which would diminish his ability to make an informed decision. We must ignore Mr Harrison's cogently argued plea to be allowed to die, if we believe it to be the product of a disturbed or clinically depressed mind.'

Judge Wyler pauses, and glances first at Emerson and then at Ken. Ken has not taken his eyes from the judge during the summing up, nor does he now.

'However I am satisfied that Mr Harrison is a brave and thoughtful man who is in complete possession of his mental faculties, and I therefore order that he be ... set free.'

With this the Judge puts his papers into shape and drops them into his briefcase, smiles benignly at those around him, and walks round to the table to where Ken is sitting, smiling broadly.

'Well, you got your hanging judge.'

'You said you were a hanging judge either way. I think not. Thank you. Thank you very much, *your Honour.*'

'Goodbye,' says Wyler.

'Goodbye sir.'

As the Judge leaves the library, Ken takes great gulps of air, and leans his head back on his pillow, eyes shut. There is a bustle of activity around him, scraping chairs, shards of conversation, rustling of papers. Carter Hill looks at Ken and wonders what he can say to his successful client. It occurs to him that the outcome of the case has just saved the insurance company a very great deal of money. He will no doubt receive a hefty bonus and an invitation to the president's country club. Ironic.

'Thanks, Carter,' says Ken, 'you're a good lawyer.'

'A lawyer is only as good as his client.'

'And as the law. It's a good law.'

'The laws are only as good as the people who make them. You're a precedent now, Ken. Goodbye.'

A precedent. Then there will be others. This is something which has not occurred to Ken.

John has hold of the wheelchair and is pushing him out of the library. 'First time I've ever known you lost for words,' says Ken.

'I'll think of something.'

They pass Claire Scott. She is smiling and frowning at the same time. She stretches out an arm.

'It's all right, Claire, it's all right.'

In the corridor Emerson joins them. While the case was on somebody has been hanging up

Christmas decorations even earlier this year. There are paper-chains and holly wreaths, and a tree, untinselled as yet and retaining its dignity. He walks alongside Ken so that they can face each other while speaking.

'Where will you go?'

'I'll get a room somewhere.'

'There's no need.'

'Dr Emerson,' says Ken, and there's a hint of anger in his voice. 'Don't start it again.'

'No, no ... You can stay here. We'll stop all treatment. No dialysis. We'll even stop feeding if you like. You'll be in a coma in a few days, dead in a week, two at the most. But there'll be little discomfort, and you'll not be alone.'

'You promise there'll be no last minute resuscitation?'

'Only if you ask for it.'

'All right. Yes. Thank you.'

Ken has not thought much about where he would go if he won his case. He presumed that he would move back to the studio, but of course that would not have done. People might have come to buy pictures; and Pat would have been there. No, that would not have done at all. A hotel room? No hotel would have him. His father's house? No. He would have liked to have gone to the sculpture and watched the children play there, but he would have frightened them off; that would not have done either. When one thinks about it, considering that Emerson has just been defeated, a defeat which presumably he would have to excuse or justify before the hospital board, Emerson is being remarkably kind.

'Why are you doing this?'

'You might change your mind.'

Ken smiles and shakes his head. They have reached his room; it seems pleasantly familiar. John pushes him into it. At once Ken is overcome with weariness, an exhaustion such as he has never before experienced. John lifts him from his chair into the bed, a job which he has never before undertaken alone, and which runs directly counter to hospital rules. Then John removes Ken's robe. Before covering his body with the sheet and blankets he impulsively plays the Steelies theme tune on the xylophone of Ken's ribs. He sings gently and almost like a lullaby:

> The sweetest girl I ever saw
> is my baby when she's in the raw
> In the raw ...

' "Raw, raw, raw," ' sings Ken in a voice so soft it is scarcely audible.

' "In the raw ..." '

' "Raw, raw, raw." '

Then both together join in the chorus:

> Punkette nights and pretty lights
> Love them ladies dressed in white.

'Thanks, John,' says Ken, as the orderly covers him.

Dr Scott comes in.

'Holy shit,' says John, and makes himself scarce.

When Claire reaches the bed, Ken sees that her face is streaked with tears. He summons all his strength to say:

'Don't. Please. Better not, I think.'

EPILOGUE
MOVING ON

Emerson was as good as his word. No attempts were made to try to persuade Ken to change his mind, and food was brought to him regularly as it had been before the hearing. But Ken had little appetite for it. Rodriguez brought him some pills which were kept within his reach, along with a paper cup of water. These, she said, he could take as and when he wished. They were analgesic and would ease any discomfort. If he needed something stronger he was to ring for it. Otherwise he was undisturbed. No therapy, no dialysis, no visits from well-meaning social workers or students. He asked Rodriguez to keep Mary Jo away from him, and preferred not to have nurses coming in every two hours to change his position. By the time any bedsores developed he would be beyond caring. For the first couple of days he needed help when he felt the need to urinate or defecate; after that his bladder and bowels no longer troubled him. He asked for the television cameras above his bed to be switched off, and so they were.

By the third day he was left entirely alone and was glad of it. Briefly he wondered whether he should ask to see Lissa, his young friend from the dialysis room. There were things he could have told her which might, he felt, have been of use to her. But she was shortly to leave the hospital. Let her live her own life. Besides, his voice was growing so faint and the effort of continuing a conversation would have been so great that he preferred things this way. Lissa would be all right.

The curtains were kept drawn, but, during the daytime enough light filtered through them to enable him to see the Hand of God in all its beauty. One day there must have been a lot of snow, for the light through the curtains had a curious quality, a kind of muted brilliance, and there were sounds of children fighting and laughing in the gardens below the window. He was extremely happy, and regretted nothing.

To begin with, his brain seemed peculiarly clear. By concentrating his mind on one thing at a time he was able to find the answers to questions which had puzzled him all his life. He found the attention which most people around him paid to the minutiae of living (and he himself had been amongst the worst) ridiculous. To begin with too he was deeply resentful of any interruptions. The screech of tyres, the distant ring of a telephone, a quarrel between nurses. Had they no consideration for him that they broke so violently into his reverie? Later he came not to mind and even to welcome these interruptions. They were part of a pattern which no longer included him. He found them quite charming, but irrelevant.

It was the same with physical discomforts. At first he was frustrated by a slight ringing in his ears, by a mouth ulcer, by an itch on the side of his nose. There was a time when these matters would have been quickly and efficiently dealt with. Now he preferred to take one of the pills and wait for the discomfort to ease. Later he stopped taking the pills. The pain, like the interruptions, was irrelevant.

A strange phenomenon. He began to think that he could feel his body again. At the very least he could remember what it was like before the accident. He remembered (and that was not so very different from feeling) the texture of skin beneath his fingers, and of grass beneath his feet. But, although at times he fancied that he was aware of his body, it was as though that body had no substance, as though it was so light that it might float away with him.

Always, when fear of what was to come threatened to overwhelm him, he focussed his eyes on the Hand of God. He could not see the rest of the room so clearly now, the shadows were growing deeper, and the outlines fainter, but this plaster hand retained its brightness, seemed almost to grow brighter, until it was hard for him to look away from it, had he wished to, which, towards the end, he no longer did.

It seemed to him sometimes that he could reach out his hands towards it and touch it. It was air and light and space, and he was a part of it.

A WAY TO DIE

ROSEMARY AND VICTOR ZORZA

At the age of twenty-five Jane Zorza learnt that she had cancer. Five months later she died. This is her story.

Rosemary and Victor Zorza tell their daughter's story vividly and frankly, without disguising their own or her thoughts and emotions. Jane's illness took an exceptionally cruel form and her family had to watch her suffer the appalling isolation of chronic pain, beyond the reach of hospital treatment or of their own love. The discovery of a hospice – one of those still too few places where highly trained doctors and nurses, acknowledging the imminence of death, concentrate on easing physical discomfort and giving real emotional support – save them from despair.

Step by step, the hospice defeated Jane's pain, then enabled her to be calm, even happy, up to the moment when she simply and acceptingly ceased to live. Meanwhile her family learnt how to help her, and gained from her in return – perhaps the most amazing part of the story – even more than they gave.

BIOGRAPHY   0 7221 9443 9   £1.50

MARY

by Patricia Collins

A CHILD YOU'LL WANT TO REMEMBER.

Mary Collins was a really beautiful baby. Born prematurely, she had a tiny oval face, a rosebud mouth and an enchanting smile. The third child of parents who came from the bustle of New York to make a home in Ireland, Mary found a warm and secure place in the heart of the family.

Then, eight months later, Patricia Collins learned that Mary was brain damaged. Doctors diagnosed cerebral palsy; she would probably never walk and she would almost certainly be retarded.

The shock of this discovery plunged Patricia into despair. Mary needed extensive therapy and the burden of caring for her increased Patricia's growing resentment and guilt — she began to drink heavily, blaming herself for what had happened. When circumstances forced the Collins family to return to America, Patricia made a wrenching decision to leave Mary behind in Ireland in a residential home for two years. The years in Ireland did nothing to lessen the severity of Mary's disabilities, but another kind of change did occur. Mary was becoming a determined, courageous child with a winning personality and she gave a very special purpose and meaning to life.

This is an intimate, inspiring and deeply moving account of a mother's journey from despair to joy and of the power of the human spirit to overcome adversity through love and understanding.

A STORY YOU WON'T FORGET.

BIOGRAPHY   0 7221 2482 1   £1.50

ENID
HARLOW

CRASHING is the extraordinarily compelling
story of Sara Richardson, a woman who has
it all. Her husband, Harry, is a successful
physician, her children are normal and healthy, she has
plenty of money, an expensive home – and a full-blown
amphetamine addiction.

For Sara, the merry-go-round of living has become a
painful ordeal which she faces daily. The pressures of
coping with a self-sufficient husband, demanding children,
and a promising career sacrificed on the altars of
marriage and motherhood, drive Sara down the path of
self-destruction. A path that leads to disaster beyond her
wildest nightmares, sending Sara crashing back to reality
and the chance to come to terms with herself.

GENERAL FICTION   0 7221 4491 1   £1.25

A MATTER OF LIFE

by Robert Edwards and Patrick Steptoe

THE MIRACLE OF THE CENTURY

On July 25th 1978, Louise Brown, the world's first test tube baby, was born. This dramatic medical breakthrough, which was hailed in every country throughout the world, was the climax of ten years of painstaking research and often heart-breaking trial and error by two doctors – gynaecologist Patrick Steptoe and scientist Robert Edwards.

In their book they reveal the secrets of their long collaboration, a unique example of co-operation between consultant and scientist, the hospital ward and the laboratory. They describe their lengthy struggles and the opposition which they encountered from religious groups, official sources, even their own profession. Above all, they tell the story of Louise Brown from the moment that Patrick Steptoe secured a mature egg from the ovary of Mrs Lesley Brown, who was infertile, to the fertilisation of the egg under laboratory conditions. And finally, nine months later came the triumphant delivery by Caesarean section and the Browns held the normal, healthy daughter they had longed for.

Extraordinary, fascinating and compelling, A MATTER OF LIFE is a testimony to the sheer determination of two doctors to bring hope and joy to thousands of childless couples throughout the world – it is, without doubt, a miracle in the history of medicine.

AUTOBIOGRAPHY   0 7221 8173 6   £1.50

A SELECTION OF BESTSELLERS FROM SPHERE

FICTION

THE HEIRLOOM	Graham Masterton	£1.25	☐
MALIBU COLONY	Pamela Wallace	£1.50	☐
EXPECTING MIRACLES	Linda Howard	£1.50	☐
I, SAID THE SPY	Derek Lambert	£1.75	☐
HEART OF WAR	John Masters	£1.95	☐

FILM & TV TIE-INS

FORT APACHE, THE BRONX	Heywood Gould	£1.75	☐
OUTLAND	Alan Dean Foster	£1.50	☐
GOODBYE DARLING	James Mitchell	95p	☐
THE PROFESSIONALS	Ken Blake	£1.00	☐
THE EMPIRE STRIKES BACK	Donald F. Glut	£1.00	☐

NON-FICTION

PEARS ENCYCLOPAEDIA OF CHILD HEALTH	Drs. Andrew & Penny Stanway	£4.95	☐
EMMA V.I.P.	Sheila Hocken	£1.25	☐
THE SPECIAL YEARS	Val Doonican	£1.25	☐
A WAY TO DIE	Rosemary & Victor Zorza	£1.50	☐
MARY	Patricia Collins	£1.50	☐

All Sphere books are available at your local bookshop or newsagent, or can be ordered direct from the publisher. Just tick the titles you want and fill in the form below.

Name _____

Address _____

_____

Write to Sphere Books, Cash Sales Department, P.O. Box 11, Falmouth, Cornwall TR10 9EN

Please enclose a cheque or postal order to the value of the cover price plus:

UK: 40p for the first book, 18p for the second book and 13p for each additional book ordered to a maximum charge of £1.49.

OVERSEAS: 60p for the first book plus 18p per copy for each additional book.

BFPO & EIRE: 40p for the first book, 18p for the second book plus 13p per copy for the next 7 books, thereafter 7p per book.

Sphere Books reserve the right to show new retail prices on covers which may differ from those previously advertised in the text or elsewhere, and to increase postal rates in accordance with the PO.